THE FAR FAR BETTER THING

By Auston Habershaw

Saga of the Redeemed
The Oldest Trick
No Good Deed
Dead But Once
The Far Far Better Thing

THE FAR FAR BETTER THING

Saga of the Redeemed: Book IV

AUSTON HABERSHAW

HARPER
VOYAGER
IMPULSE

An Imprint of HarperCollinsPublishers

THE FAR FAR BETTER THING. Copyright © 2019 by Auston Habershaw. All rights reserved. Printed in the United States of America. No part of this book may be used or reproduced in any manner whatsoever without written permission except in the case of brief quotations embodied in critical articles and reviews. For information, address HarperCollins Publishers, 195 Broadway, New York, NY 10007.

Digital Edition MARCH 2019 ISBN: 978-0-06-267703-7
Print Edition ISBN: 978-0-06-267705-1

Cover design by Patricia Barrow
Cover photographs © taviphoto/iStock/Getty Images (antler); ©Ron-Tech2000/iStock/Getty Images (throne); © TeoLazarev/iStock/Getty Images (smoke)

Harper Voyager, the Harper Voyager logo, and Harper Voyager Impulse are trademarks of HarperCollins Publishers.

HarperCollins is a registered trademark of HarperCollins Publishers in the United States of America and other countries.

FIRST EDITION

19 20 21 22 23   OPM   10 9 8 7 6 5 4 3 2 1

*This book is dedicated to
my daughters, Madelyn and Violet:
find the steel inside you, my girls,
and hone it well*

There is nothing noble in being superior to your fellow men. True nobility lies in being superior to your former self.

—ERNEST HEMINGWAY

TABLE OF CONTENTS

PROLOGUE

The Keeper of the Balance, Polimeux II, was a haggard old man with a hook nose and a bleary gaze perpetually fixed on some unknowable, distant horizon. Though he was fairly dripping with gilded amulets and precious stones and clad in thick robes of lush and vibrant purple, he had the look of a beggar mooching coppers down by the docks. This, as Xahlven understood it, was the way with Keepers. Once you achieved the fifth mark in the Chamber of Testing, you lost something of yourself. Some idiots claimed you gained some "higher understanding." Xahlven was pretty sure the only thing that "higher understanding" did was make you lose your mind.

Of course, that never stopped the raggedy old nut from looking down his ridiculous nose at Xahlven. "You are late, young Xahlven."

Xahlven, in point of fact, was *not* late. It just so happened that the other four archmagi had arrived earlier than he had. Still, he put on his best sheepish grin and genuflected to the Keeper on his towering dais at the center of the chamber. "My apologies, Keeper. Time runs differently in the Black College, it seems. I lost track."

The Keeper's displeasure quickly dissipated as his attention drifted to some distant eddy of time and space. Xahlven doubted the old goat had any memory of their brief exchange, and so he took the obsidian throne reserved for the Archmage of the Ether and waited for the opening ceremonies of the meeting to run their course.

The Chamber of Stars stood at the very heart of the Arcanostrum, at the very nexus of three of the world's most powerful ley lines. It was, therefore, a place where the five great energies of existence—Ether, Lumen, Fey, Dweomer, and Astral—were in such vital abundance that they could be seen with the naked eye, pulsating through the walls along veins of precious metal long ago infused into the stones. The four quadrants of the rhomboid room each blazed with the character of their respective energies—Xahlven's part, for instance, was dark and silent, with stagnant puddles forming upon the flagstones and long, unnatural shadows.

Sitting on that ancient throne, he could feel more

power coursing through him than in any other place. It was a good thing, too—his mother's hex was still there, draining away his power at all times, day and night. A week since his duel with her in the Empty Tower, and still he had found no way to remove it. He had often been tempted to try his luck here, with all the power of the Star Chamber at his command, but then his fellow archmagi would doubtlessly notice what he was doing, and he had no intention of showing them weakness.

On the floor of the chamber, between the central dais and the platforms of each archmage, Trevard, Lord Defender of the Balance—the technical archmage of the Astral—walked a circuit of the room, verifying with various auguries that each archmage was indeed who they said they were, and not some shrouded or shape-shifted impostor, simulacrum, or other such ruse. Trevard was a tall, thin man with a severe, humorless face, his forehead creased with frown lines that extended up beneath his mageglass helm. He spent an unusually long time peering at Xahlven, verifying his identity. There was a lot of banging his staff upon the ground and grunting on the Lord Defender's part. Xahlven chose to ignore it.

When he had finished with each of the archmagi, Trevard banged his staff against the floor five times more. "The Great Cabal is complete, all are present. May the Balance prevail!"

The noise broke Polimeux from whatever stupor had transfixed his attention on his hands. "What? Yes . . . yes of course. What of Eretheria, my servants?"

Trevard started speaking almost before the Keeper had finished asking the question. "Necromancy! Necromancy used to field an army of the living dead! This cannot be tolerated!"

The Archmage of the Dweomer, Delkatar—the eldest archmage by far and a conservative relic—smoothed his knee-length beard with one hand. "A lost art, I assumed. Who has found it anew?"

"It has not been taught in the White College for centuries, of that I can assure you." Talian, the Archmage of the Lumen, was looking directly at Xahlven from the opposite side of the chamber, her rose-colored spectacles glinting in the glow of her bright and shiny quadrant. "I am *forced* to assume there has been some kind of malfeasance."

"I can't imagine why you are looking at me that way, Talian," Xahlven said. "I am as disturbed as the rest of you, and necromancy is a *Lumenal* art, remember?"

"Oh, it's just hedge magic, is all." Hugarth, Archmage of the Fey, hooked a knee over the armrest of his brass throne. "Who cares if somebody's animated a few corpses?"

"*I* care!" Trevard said, banging his staff on the floor again. "This so-called 'Gray Lady' is a former Defender who—"

Hugarth laughed. "A former Defender, eh? Well, that sounds as though it's one of those *you* problems, not a *me* problem."

Xahlven did his best not to sneer at Hugarth—even if he was taking the position Xahlven wanted, there was just something so unseemly about an archmage who didn't wear shoes. "Lord Defender," he said softly, "the issue is not whether or not Myreon Alafarr has committed a crime—of that we are all agreed, yes?"

Nods around the hall, except from Hugarth, who merely shrugged. The Keeper seemed not to be paying any attention, which suited Xahlven just fine. He continued. "The issue is how the Balance can be *best preserved*."

Delkatar banged his staff in approval. "That is sensible. This woman is the instigator of a popular revolt, but the revolt has already *been* instigated, yes? If we remove her now . . . well . . ."

"Chaos," Xahlven confirmed. "We create a martyr—"

"You mean *another* martyr," Talian broke in. She smiled sweetly at Xahlven. "The first one was your *brother*. Or . . . have you forgotten about him already?"

Xahlven barely suppressed a bark of rage. "Yes, yes—of course. *Another* martyr, very well—the *point* is that removing Alafarr won't stop the uprising, it will merely rob it of its moderating influence. The woman wants to create a better, more stable Eretheria. I propose we let her try."

Delkatar nodded while Talian looked pensive.

Hugarth jerked his chin in Xahlven's direction. "And just what are *you* getting out of this, boy?"

Carefully, carefully . . . "A stable Eretheria, Hugarth."

"*If* she wins," Delkatar said.

"*And* if she loses—then the old order will be restored." Xahlven looked around at them all. "Let her continue, because win or lose, the war ends one way or another. Necromancy or no necromancy."

"Necromancy is an *abomination!*" Trevard was livid, his nostrils flaring so wide a sparrow could conceivably get caught in one.

Xahlven couldn't let that one go. "And firepikes aren't? Colossi? Bladecrystals? War fiends? It seems the Lord Defender is perfectly satisfied with all the *other* sorcerous weapons we have permitted to propagate across the West, but when it comes to dead bodies holding spears, *there* the line is crossed?"

"Mind your manners, young man." Delkatar had the temerity to waggle a finger in Xahlven's direction, like he was some misbehaving nephew and not a fellow archmage. "It was *your mother* who brought us to this pass. Don't go blaming Trevard for your own family's misdeeds."

"And do not presume to lecture me about my own family, Delkatar," Xahlven said, keenly aware of how hot his temper was running. These . . . these *idiots*. These self-involved imbeciles! Gods, if there were only poison enough in the world to drown them all in it.

He closed his eyes and took a cleansing breath. Not yet. Not *yet*. His mother took thirty years to have her grand plot come to fruition; he could wait a few more months for his own. *One step at a time, Xahlven.* "Myreon Alafarr must remain in command of the rebel army she is massing in Eretheria. We cannot interfere without making the problem worse."

"If she maintains an army of the living dead—" Trevard began.

"Then we can warn her—threaten her. By all means we can encourage her to stop using proscribed sorcery. I am not suggesting otherwise." *Indeed*, Xahlven thought, *I very much want you to do so, you inflexible old battle-axe.*

Trevard looked up at Xahlven, thinking the suggestion over. "You know the woman. How would she react to such a threat?"

"She will not wish to anger Saldor—her rebellion cannot confront another enemy." This was not precisely a lie. But neither was it entirely true. *Myreon will do exactly what she feels she must, threats or no threats.*

Silence fell over the chamber as everyone mulled this over. Xahlven steepled his fingers beneath his chin. This was the moment he had been scrying for some time—what happened now would alter how his plans would unfold from this moment forward. No doubt his fellow archmagi, too, had scryed this. Manipulating them was the most delicate of arts, stupid though they were. It had taken him only a week as archmage to realize how much he hated them all, but it had taken him almost ten years of constant, painstaking plotting to bring them to this juncture. That they suspected nothing he felt was proof positive of his genius. Now the fools mulled over the time of their own deaths, and it was all Xahlven could do to keep from grinning.

Talian spoke first. "Agreed. As much as I dislike it, Xahlven is correct. Trevard should send her a warning, but we should take no direct action unless she escalates things."

Delkatar agreed as well, and Hugarth shrugged his shoulders and said he couldn't give a damn either way. It fell to Trevard. "I will make preparations to field an army of Defenders at short notice, just in case, but . . . but I am reluctantly forced to agree with the Archmage of the Ether."

Xahlven gave Trevard a shallow bow out of respect. The old battle-mage returned the gesture reflexively and grinned. Xahlven had seen that grin in his scrying pool before—he knew now what happened next, and knew it better than any other person in that hall. With that grin, Trevard had sealed his fate. Xahlven's plot could never be stopped now. Not by Trevard, nor by any other archmage.

For the first time in years, he saw a clear, unbroken path to victory—to an end of the perverse order of the world as fashioned by his mother and a beginning of a new era of his own devising. The board had been cleared of all obstacles—his mother, awaiting her death in Sahand's tallest tower, his brother dead and on the bottom of a lake, and Myreon Alafarr embroiled in a war she could never hope to win. No matter how his mother's hex drained his power, Xahlven couldn't help but smile.

The Keeper of the Balance, Polimeux II—the most powerful mage in the world—wiped a string of drool from his face with a silk handkerchief. "What of Eretheria, my servants?"

"Never fear, Keeper," Xahlven said. "Everything is well in hand."

CHAPTER 1

RUDE AWAKENING

Tyvian awoke with a gasp and then he kept gasping, gulping down air as though he hadn't breathed in days. He was struggling—something was grabbing him, holding him down. He kicked and thrashed and then coarse wool was thrown over his head and it was dark. He tried to scream, but his voice barely seemed to creak.

He fell out of the bed and thumped his face on a dirt floor. He was covered in a wool blanket, which had been pushed up over his head by his struggles. He lay there for a moment, collecting his wits, letting his breathing calm. *I'm alive*, he thought. *The ring brought me back*. He felt it on his right hand—cold, hard, immovable. Hard to imagine so much power packed in so plain an iron band.

The plan worked!

He was lying in a barn. There were no animals present and the big doors were pulled closed. Sunbeams through the windows lit the dust and motes of hay in the air, cutting diagonally across the big, empty room—it was either early morning or evening, then. The place smelled of horse manure and a hundred different kinds of dander. His bed was something makeshift—a couple of sacks stuffed with dirt laid atop a few small crates. A little cook fire was going, the smoke rising up above the hayloft and then out the vent near the barn's roof. Tyvian frowned at it. An open fire in a barn was a bad idea, unless . . .

The door slid open a few inches—enough for a big man with a sword on his back to slip through sideways. He was clad in black mail and had a shaggy mane of black hair striped with gray. When he turned to face Tyvian, he could see that the man had been growing his beard out again. "Well met, Eddereon."

Eddereon smiled, showing his uneven teeth. "Back with us at last, eh? I was beginning to wonder."

"Has it been two weeks?" Tyvian pulled himself atop the makeshift bed. It was now that he noted what he was wearing—a loose shirt, brown and stained, and a pair of green hose patched at the knees and toes. He nearly gagged.

"Those clothes were the best I could find—you'd better plan on keeping them." Eddereon rubbed his beard and squatted next to the fire. "It's been about twelve days since the Battle of Eretheria, which is what they're calling it. How did you know it had been—"

"Your beard," Tyvian said offhandedly as he inspected himself. The wounds were all there, barely scabbed over—each place Xahlven's simulacra had run him through. He felt the tightness of healing skin around each of them. They'd probably scar. "Who won the battle?"

Eddereon stirred a wooden spoon in the little iron cauldron he had suspended over the fire. "Depends on who you ask. The White Army insists it was a great victory for Eretheria, the Dellorans insist that it went exactly as planned, and the Free Houses will insist whatever scoops up the most popular support is the truth."

"The White Army?"

"Myreon," Eddereon said. He pulled out the spoon and licked it. "Hmph . . . I've grown too used to pepper."

Tyvian rubbed his temples, only to discover that he had no hair. Someone had shaved his head. "What . . . what the *hell?*"

Eddereon chuckled. "I know you went to a lot of trouble to fake your death, but not *everyone* believed it. Red hair is likely to stick out."

Tyvian closed his eyes and took a good, long breath. It was the right play. It made sense. But he still felt naked. His goatee, at least, was intact, if a bit ragged. "The Free Houses?"

"The war is shaping up like this: the White Army is putting any noble to the sword who doesn't join the cause and renounce their titles. Turns out this is very popular among the peasantry, who flock to the Gray Lady's banners. House Davram is likely to march on the capital, or is doing so right now—battle is in the wind. Ayventry is under the control of Sahand. That leaves Camis, Vora, and Hadda, all of whom are biding their time to see how Davram fares. Until then, they're the 'Free Houses.'"

"It didn't work, then. My death didn't unify them against Sahand."

Eddereon shrugged. "I have never been very good at politics. It seems to me, though, that if Myreon defeats Davram in the field, the western part of the country will stay at peace—Camis and Vora seem unlikely to get involved, and Hadda will stay neutral until a winner seems clear. That just leaves Sahand."

"Half a war is still a war. And Sahand is better at it than Myreon is."

Eddereon spooned out a brown-black stew of beans and some kind of game meat into a wooden bowl and shoved it in Tyvian's hands. "Begging your pardon, but none of that is your concern any longer, correct? That man—Tyvian Reldamar—he's dead. You're somebody else now."

Tyvian thought about this as he cast about for his

own spoon. "Eddereon, do you by any chance happen to have—"

"New person, remember?" Eddereon held up one hand and wiggled his fingers at Tyvian. "Learn to adapt."

Tvyian cursed and looked down at the stew. It was thick and hot and he realized just how hungry he was. "Dammit all." He pulled out a piece of meat and stuffed it in his mouth. It was tough, but good. Its taste made him remember all those meals Hool had hunted down during their vagabond years. He wondered where she was and if she was well. He wondered if Brana was with her.

"Once you've eaten, you'll need to put on this." Eddereon went into a stall and came back with a pair of boots, a thick gray tunic of wool, a mail shirt and coif, a sword belt with a broadsword, and a black tabard with an elk-skull device, the antlers reaching almost to the collar.

Tyvian looked at it—this had been the plan. "What company are we with?"

Eddereon tapped the device on the tabard. "This is the sign of Rodall's Hunters, also called the Ghouls. They are camped not far away and are waiting for me—a personal favor."

Tyvian poked through the outfit, paying particular attention to the sword. It was competently made, but not the work of a master. It would need a lot of sharpening. "You know them?"

"We know each other by reputation," Eddereon said. "Whereas you were something of a legend in your circle, I was something of a legend in mine. Few sell-swords do not know the name of Eddereon the Black."

Tyvian picked out a bit more stew, resisting the urge to reach for a napkin. "And who am I?"

"Arick Cadronmay of Denthro, hedge knight and my bosom companion, just recovered from his injuries at the Battle of Eretheria."

Tyvian pulled on the boots. They were well worn, but again of decent construction. They fit, too—Eddereon had a good eye for sizes.

Conversation died as Tyvian ate and dressed. He would have liked to bathe, but this being a barn, no tub was present, and he sure as hell wasn't about to scrub down in a feed trough. Sacrifices needed to be made, he supposed. First his hair, then his hygiene.

Why was he doing all this, again? He stopped as he was belting on the broadsword, suddenly alarmed at a gap in his memory. He cast his mind back, trying to confirm all the details. He remembered everything leading up to his coronation with relative clarity, but the night of the ordeal itself . . . well . . . he remembered fire and death and his duel with Xahlven on the rooftop. But how had he gotten there? What else had happened?

He frowned. There was something there. Something on the edge of his memory . . . something Xahlven had told him, right at the end. Something important.

He pushed the thought away. It didn't matter anymore, did it? He was done—free. He'd sacrificed himself for Eretheria, and now the rest of the world and its problems were no longer his own. He wasn't Tyvian the First, he wasn't even Tyvian Reldamar. He was Arick Cadronmay of Denthro, disgraced hedge knight—a common sell-sword and no one of consequence. Tyvian took a deep, cleansing breath.

For the first time in ages—decades, perhaps— Tyvian's life seemed to unfold before him with wild, unrestricted promise.

Eddereon was standing at the barn door. He cleared his throat. "We'd better go. They won't wait much longer."

Tyvian nodded and finished belting on the sword. It seemed too heavy, and it dragged on his hip. He'd never much cared for broadswords—they were balanced more toward the tip than the hilt to give them a heavier stroke, but when compared to his preferred rapier, you lost a measure of control and a few inches of reach. He hoped those few inches and that extra control wouldn't matter much. Given the arc of his life thus far, that didn't seem likely. "Very well. Let's go."

The camp of Rodall's Hunters was a typical sell-sword encampment. It straddled a road on the north side of a stream crossed by a narrow stone bridge. A cheval-de-frise was placed across the bridge on both sides, and it was manned by a half-dozen men clad as Tyvian was and armed with long spears and bows. Beyond this, the tents were arranged in neat rows, and a central pavilion of black and white flew the company colors and had the company standard staked out front—a larger, more detailed version of the device on Tyvian's chest, this including streaks of blood dripping from the antlers and a border stitched with the images of human skulls. Not cheery, but then again, sell-swords traded on their fearsome reputations, and fearsome banners helped keep them in coin.

Eddereon greeted the men on the bridge by name and they let him pass with some slaps on the back and good-natured ribbing about farmer's daughters and so on. They didn't say a word to Tyvian at all.

As they walked through the camp, Tyvian spared a look at the tents. They were small, housing four men apiece, though Tyvian guessed the men would have to be stacked like firewood inside if everyone were to sleep at once. There was precious little magecraft in evidence: the tents were not warded against the elements, the cook fires were stoked with plain wood, and only a few of the men's weapons had the telltale sheen of having been treated with bladecrystal. That meant the company was either low on supplies or perhaps poor. In either case, Tyvian didn't expect much in the way of comfort.

The men were in the process of striking camp.

They knew their duties and they did them, rolling up tents and loading supply wagons in organized teams. Tyvian found himself counting fingers, ears, noses, and eyes—he came up with less than the expected number. Far less, and most of the injuries were not recent. These were veterans, then, not some green company out of Galaspin looking to make some quick coin in the spring campaigns. Tyvian, with his well-fed complexion and a full set of digits, was going to stick out here.

"Cheery bunch," Tyvian grumbled to Eddereon as a man with no teeth and shoulders like a bull glared at him. "You could have found a less . . . conspicuous group, couldn't you?"

"I did the best that I could. The Ghouls will do," Eddereon said and led on, heading toward the central pavilion. Beside the elaborate banner was a pair of guards standing at attention, halberds at their sides.

Tyvian ducked past a pair of men carrying five rolled-up tents between them. "Why are they called the Ghouls?"

"The Siege of Gandor's Gate."

Tyvian tried to remember his history. "That was at the end of the Illini Wars, after Calassa, right? Sahand's men held the castle for two months and started eating their captives . . . but why would *this* company be called the Ghouls if it was the Dellorans who were eating . . ."

Eddereon stopped and gave Tyvian a hard stare over his shoulder.

Tyvian came up short. The realization hit him like a wave—the Dellorans were falling back *north* in front of the White Army. The Ghouls were camped on the *north* side of the river, guarding their southern approaches. Gods. *This is a Delloran Company!*

I'm joining Sahand's service!

When Eddereon saw that Tyvian understood, he nodded and introduced himself to the guards at the front of the pavilion. He was seen inside, but Tyvian was told to remain here. He did as he was told, if only because he was too shocked to think of another thing to do. They were in a Delloran camp! He kept darting his eyes around, expecting at any moment for one of the sundry thugs and murderers surrounding him to notice who he was and sound the alert. Nothing happened, though—the tabard, his shaved head, and the fact that his ordeal probably had adverse effects on his appearance were sufficient to confound anyone who might happen to recognize him, even assuming such a person existed.

But what if such a person did? He might pass casual inspection, but how long until his Saldorian accent gave him away? Did Sahand believe he was dead? Hard to say—it wasn't Sahand he was attempting to fool. What were the odds they would come into Sahand's presence?

What in the hell was Eddereon *thinking*?

A pair of huge wolfhounds emerged from the pavilion, wearing spiked collars. They did not wag their tails or pant or even come close to Tyvian. Instead, they both stared at him with black eyes, stone-still. Tyvian also froze, uncertain what to do. He glanced at the two guards standing there, but neither man said or did anything.

Laughter filtered out of the pavilion and into the morning sun. The man Eddereon was with had a head like a whetstone—gray, with nothing but sharp corners and flat surfaces. He wore plate-and-mail of good quality, and his head was shaved in the manner of knights who still wore a helm on a regular basis. His teeth, evidently worn down with age, had each been capped with platinum crowns. Though half a head shorter than Eddereon, he bore a kind of violent menace that made Tyvian feel he was bigger. He gave the two hounds a low whistle, and the dogs instantly sat at his heels. Their eyes still hadn't left Tyvian.

"Arick Cadronmay of Denthro," Eddereon said, presenting Tyvian, "meet Captain Rodall Gern."

Tyvian knuckled his forehead in salute and bowed for good measure—he was abruptly realizing he had no idea what the etiquette was here. Should he kneel? Would he be kissing rings?

Captain Rodall extended his hand to shake. Tyvian grabbed his forearm and Rodall squeezed his—too hard. "Well met," Rodall said, his voice far higher pitched than Tyvian had expected out of such a face.

"Milord," Tyvian answered.

Rodall hooted a laugh. "You weren't kidding, Ed—high-born and polite. I'm worried I might break him!"

"No danger of that, sir!" Tyvian said, trying to sound more eager than he was.

"Arrogant, too." Rodall shook his head. "On any other day, I'd break your knees and leave a ponce like you behind for the crows. I lost too many men in that shit-eating town full of wigs and women, though, to pass up free help. Can you handle a pike?"

Tyvian nodded. Any moron could handle a pike—what kind of stupid question was that? Still, he couldn't resist a follow up question. "Free, sir?"

Rodall looked at Eddereon. "Thought you told him?"

Eddereon stepped in. "You don't get paid in Rodall's Hunters until you're blooded in your first battle. Gives new recruits an incentive to stick the engagement out rather than run."

Rodall came close to Tyvian and stared down his flat nose. "And once you're blooded, you're *ours*—no deserters in this company, understood? You take off without my leave, and I hunt you down."

Tyvian did his best not to roll his eyes. If he had a copper common every time somebody threatened to hunt him down . . .

"Not impressed, eh?" Rodall yanked out a piece

of Tyvian's beard, making Tyvian wince. He held the hair out to his hounds, which eagerly sniffed it. He then stuffed the little sprig of hair into his belt.

"They know you now, boy," Rodal said, grinning his metal-capped grin. "If you run, well . . ." He reached up to his neck and teased out a leather string that wove through a half dozen mummified human ears. "We'll see how brave you are when I catch you."

Rodall looked at Eddereon, slapped a hand on his shoulder, and nodded. "I need to get back—got a company to run. You're both in tent twenty-five. Would make you sergeant, but the boys would take it wrong, some stranger riding their rumps."

Eddereon saluted. "Of course. Thank you, sir."

Tyvian spoke up, "Hold on—tent twenty-five? I'm . . . errr . . . *we're* to march with the infantry?"

Rodall paused. "We're an infantry company—what the hell else would you do?"

"Well, sir—it seems to me that a man leading a company abroad through enemy territory could use a guide."

"I could cross rougher terrain than this in my sleep," Rodall said. But he turned around and folded his arms—he was listening, at any rate.

Tyvian was getting a death-stare from Eddereon, but he pressed on anyway. "I don't mean the *physical* terrain. I mean the *political* terrain. I know this country—I know its people and its laws. I might be useful to you in the command tent." Deathly silence from Rodall. Then Tyvian remembered to add the word "Sir."

Rodall favored Tyvian with another shiny grin. "Maybe you would at that. Very well, Arick—you will report to my command tent each evening after camp has been set. Understood?"

Tyvian saluted. "Yes sir."

And then Rodall and his giant dogs went back in the pavilion, leaving them alone save the guards. Eddereon put an arm around Tyvian's shoulder and steered him away. "You made a good impression. Well done."

Tyvian hissed at him. "Sahand's service, Eddereon? *Sahand?* Kroth's teeth, man, what were you thinking?"

"Shhh . . . I can explain."

"Explain bloody well quick, you great hairy oaf!"

Eddereon cast a look around—the bustle of the camp was intensifying. There were horns blowing, and men scrambled to load wagons and shoulder their packs. No one was paying them any heed. "Your plan has changed a bit, Tyvian."

Tyvian smacked him in the side of the head. "Call me Arick, you dunce—and who told you to change any plans! The idea was to get out of Eretheria and then we'd lie low. Travelling with the enemy is *not* lying low!"

Eddereon grimaced and sought to explain, but the

big man was having trouble finding the words. "Your mother . . . after the battle . . . she . . . well . . . she was captured by Sahand."

The news hit Tyvian harder than he expected. *She's dead.* He took a step back. A thousand methods of painful, torturous death flashed through his mind, each of them a potential fate for his mother. He wondered which of them it had been, or maybe Sahand hadn't bothered choosing and did them all. He wondered where the body was being displayed. He shook his head. "She . . . when she told me that was the last time we'd speak, I . . . I didn't believe her."

Eddereon took Tyvian by the shoulders. "No, you don't understand. Your mother is *alive*, held captive in Dellor."

Tyvian blinked. "What? Wh . . . why?"

Eddereon seemed not to hear the question. "We have joined the Delloran army because you and I are going to rescue her."

That's insane. Tyvian didn't get a chance to say it, though. The horns were blowing. They were being called into ranks. Rodall's Hunters—the Ghouls of Dellor—were marching north.

And Tyvian was going with them.

CHAPTER 2

IN THE ARMY NOW

Marching, Tyvian quickly discovered, was unpleasant. The Ghouls—nobody in the company called them the Hunters unless the captain was in earshot—were a light infantry outfit evidently famed for their ability to cover ground quickly. The departure from their camp that first morning was considered leisurely by company standards, even though to Tyvian it had looked as though they were striking tents while people were still sleeping in them.

Somebody shoved a pike in Tyvian's hand—an eighteen-foot-long spear that weighed about eight pounds—and slapped a pack on his back that contained a blanket roll, a quantity of dry rations, a canteen, and some assortment of camping knickknacks Tyvian did not have the time to inspect. Over this pack, that same somebody hung a small target shield and yelled at him until Tyvian was standing in a column with other people with absurdly long spears and large packs.

They were then made to walk. For hours. Eight hours, specifically, with only a brief midday respite to choke down a few iron-hard crackers and a handful of seeds before they were once again bellowed at until they were back in lines, marching again. By midday, Tyvian's legs were screaming with exhaustion. By dusk, they were just numb.

There was very little conversation among the men while marching. Everyone was focused on keeping pace, since the sergeant—the man who had apparently made it his life's mission to scream at Tyvian for any minor infraction—was pacing the edge of the column. He was a toothless badger of a human being with scraggly yellow hair that grew just about everywhere on his head except the top. His name was Drawsher. In another life, Tyvian would have killed him five minutes after meeting him. In this life—this wretched, reduced, quasiexistence he now occupied—he was Tyvian's immediate superior.

"You! Fancy boy! Quit yer lagging!" Drawsher shouted in Tyvian's ear as though Tyvian were deaf. He cracked Tyvian across the backside with a slender rod. A white-hot line of pain bloomed, making Tyvian wince.

"Oy, you think that hurt, Duchess?" Drawsher snarled. "It'll hurt worse'n that if you don't keep pace, damn your lazy arse!"

"I *am* keeping pace," Tyvian grumbled.

"*Quiet in the ranks!*" Drawsher screamed and hit Tyvian three more times, all across the arse or the back of his legs.

The urge to club the brute over the head with his pike was enormous. Even the ring was ambivalent about it, as it often was in cases of self-defense. But Tyvian clenched his teeth and picked up the pace slightly. Drawsher, evidently satisfied, moved on to find other victims. It turned out there was always *somebody* in the Ghouls who had an arse that needed a few strikes.

Tyvian was not a perfect judge of such things, but when the command came to set camp, he was reasonably certain they'd gone about twenty-five miles in a single day. Tyvian had scarcely been in such a rush in his entire life, and *he'd* been hunted by the Defenders of the Balance across half a continent.

Compared to marching, setting camp was also unpleasant, but in an entirely different way. Drawsher singled Tyvian and a handful of other "bones"—a Ghoul term for raw recruits—to dig a latrine. Tyvian made the argument that the captain had ordered him to his tent each evening after they camped.

Dawsher was unimpressed. "If'n the captain wants to talk to you, then I'm a honey-glazed ham!"

The analogy garnered a hearty laugh from Tyvian's new "companions." This, evidently, was what passed for humor among the Ghouls.

Tyvian was too fatigued to be snarky at that precise moment, but he did devise some choice insults for later deployment while hacking at the rocky Eretherian ground with a glorified garden trowel referred to as an "entrenching tool." It was, evidently, one of those pointless pieces of military paraphernalia that Tyvian had previously given little notice to, but now constituted the majority of his waking thoughts.

It was there, digging a ditch in the dying daylight, that Tyvian formally met his new social circle. Now no longer in ranks and with Sergeant Drawsher nowhere in sight, the Delloran mercenaries began to chatter. The first thing that struck Tyvian about them was their age—he guessed he was at least fifteen years older than all of them. He knew it made sense—it *shouldn't* have surprised him, given he was about their age when he joined up with Carlo diCarlo's pirate crew—but there was something inescapably jarring in realizing he was, in the eyes of the young, an old man.

An additional obstacle to forging any new alliances was that all of these young men were immensely, incurably stupid. They were young men from Dellor, and sometimes Galaspin, who had found marching to Eretheria with the Ghouls a more productive use of their lives than herding cows, breaking rocks, or coaxing plants out of the ground. Unless it had something to do with one of those three activities, they knew exactly nothing about anything.

They disliked Tyvian immediately. His alias, as it turned out, was utterly unnecessary, as Sergeant Drawsher had seen to it that nobody would ever use his name again. He was "Duchess" for now and ever.

"Oy, Duchess!" Hambone, a fat boy of perhaps twenty from Dellor who had been blabbering steadily about his family pig farm, was working his yard-long entrenching tool like it was a murder implement and his victim the earth itself. "Gimme a hand over here!"

Tyvian felt about as motivated to assist Hambone as he would be a urine-soaked street person. "You need to *scoop* the dirt, Hambone. Stop making holes and start actually digging."

Some of the other bones snickered. Hambone threw down his tool. "I done more ditch digging before I was ten than you done your whole fat life!"

Tyvian's tool bounced off a stone. He kicked the stone aside. "And yet you remain terrible at it. Some would call that a miracle."

Hambone came closer. Despite evidently having marched hundreds of miles from Dellor, he somehow had never lost the stench of pigs. "You think you're better than me, Duchess?"

Tyvian looked him in the eye. "Yes. In every field of endeavor, from now until the day you die."

The ring twinged softly, warning Tyvian against

hitting the boy. Tyvian didn't, knowing full well the idiot was going to hit him first.

Or try.

Hambone stood there, fists clenched, fuming. Behind him, some of the other bones egged him on. "Knock him good, Hammy! Piss on his lordship's arse!"

Tyvian waited. "Well, are you going to try and urinate on my arse, or what?"

Hambone swung. Even though monstrously tired from marching, Tyvian ducked the blow easily and ended the fight in as expeditious a method as possible—he hit Hambone in the knee with his entrenching tool. Not hard—just hard enough to make the boy's leg buckle and for it to hurt *really* badly. Hambone fell on his back in the muddy depths of the latrine ditch, howling.

The ring stayed mercifully silent.

The other bones backed away from him, their eyes wide. "Weren't no call for that," one of them muttered.

Tyvian ignored Hambone's groans. "You've joined a company of hired killers called 'The Ghouls,' for Hann's sake! How much bloody fair play did you expect?"

Hambone flopped, trying to stand, but his knee gave way immediately and he fell back in the half-dug latrine. "Help! Oh gods, me leg! Ohhhh!"

This time the ring *did* have an opinion. It gave Tyvian a hard jolt that snapped him out of his staring contest with the other fresh recruits. "Oh . . . very well, dammit."

He slipped an arm under Hambone's armpit and helped him to his feet. Tyvian took a look at his injured knee. It was bulging and swollen—Tyvian guessed he'd maybe knocked the kneecap out of alignment or possibly dislocated the whole joint, though he didn't think he'd swung that hard. Hambone leaned heavily on Tyvian's shoulders—appropriately enough, he seemed to weigh as much as a prize hog. "It hurts! Ohhhh!"

Grimacing, Tyvian walked the idiot to Eddereon, who was examining the blisters growing on one foot outside their tiny tent. He stood as they approached. "What's all this?"

Tears were rolling down Hambone's flat cheeks. "He hit me! Ohhh! Right in the knee!"

Eddereon looked at Tyvian. "Well?"

Tyvian only nodded. "I hit him. Right in the knee."

"You better get him to the medical tent before Drawsher sees."

"Sees what?" Drawsher emerged from behind a pike stand like a troll lumbering out of a hedge. "What happened here?"

Eddereon and Tyvian exchanged quick glances. "An accident, sir. Digging the latrine."

Drawsher looked at the three of them, scratching at his unkempt beard. "Accident, is it? Hey, Hambone—can you walk?"

Hambone shook his head, tears still streaming down his cheeks.

"I can help him to the medical tent, sir," Tyvian offered.

Drawsher laughed in Tyvian's face. "What for? Man can't walk—he's useless. We leave him behind come dawn."

The color drained from Hambone's face. "What? You can't! You can't leave me here!"

Drawsher leaned close to Hambone, as though about to whisper something conspiratorial. Instead, he sucker punched Hambone in the lower abdomen, folding the fat man in half like a bath towel. Nearby, a few other mercenaries laughed.

The ring blazed on Tyvian's hand. "You miserable son of a—"

Drawsher had a dagger out in a flash and pressed it under Tyvian's nose. "Am I going to get lip from you, Duchess? Eh?" He dragged the blade gently along Tyvian's mouth. "If I am, I might as well *take em now*, eh?"

Tyvian kept his eyes on Drawsher's eyes. The play with the knife was scary, sure, but also wildly stupid. Tyvian could have put that knife in Drawsher's own throat in two moves, three tops. His fingers twitched, wanting to. How many two-bit bullies like Drawsher had Tyvian put in the ground? Gods, too many to even bother counting. If there was a reason he was better at digging holes than Hambone, it was because of all the bodies he'd buried over the years.

But I'm not Tyvian anymore, he cautioned himself. *Play the damned part.*

Tyvian let his eyes drop from Drawsher's. "There were wounded riding in a wagon today. I saw them. Why can't Hambone ride, too, sir?"

Drawsher withdrew the knife. He nodded. "Them's blooded men—them's true Ghouls, Duchess. This here bone would be wasted space. Space we need for supplies, for armor—for things what matter."

Tyvian looked down at Hambone, who was still wheezing and moaning on the ground. "What if I carry his load? What if I make up the space that he takes?"

Drawsher cocked his head. "Well now . . . ain't that noble of you, Duchess. Downright gentlemanly." He slapped his knife home in its scabbard. "All right, then—bring him to the healer. But you carry his pack tomorrow, Duchess. And his pike. And *anything else I say.*"

There was mirth in Drawsher's bloodshot eyes. Tyvian nodded—he knew what it meant for him tomorrow. He licked his lips. "As you say, sir."

Drawsher grinned. "Another wrong breath from you, Duchess, and I'll eat your kidneys, understand?"

Tyvian saluted as best he could. Drawsher went back to his rounds.

Eddereon patted Tyvian on the shoulder. "You certainly have a way with people sometimes."

Tyvian didn't answer. He helped Hambone up.

Hambone, pale, managed to say, "What in hell is wrong with you, Duchess? You trying to get dead?"

"Tried, Hambone. Tried and succeeded."

The camp doctor—a hedge wizard and probably non-guild alchemist named Rink—managed to relocate Hambone's kneecap and put the man's leg in a splint. It was the back of a wagon for Hambone for one week. Tyvian, meanwhile, carried double the weight, plus a five-gallon water skin slung over one shoulder.

Despite his inquiries, there was no indication of him being invited to Rodall's command tent. Sergeant Drawsher had Tyvian all to himself.

The first day, Drawsher circled him like a raven. The weight was overwhelming, the pace punishing—the sergeant was expecting a long day of beating the snot out of Tyvian Reldamar. The ring, though, had a few things to say about that. Saving Hambone from abandonment was enough to keep Tyvian upright and marching, the ring's power driving every step. He was still exhausted, still punishing his body in ways he'd never considered possible before, but he kept up. Drawsher barely had an excuse to strike him.

So, in a fit of pique, he assigned Tyvian latrine duty *alone* for three days straight.

Despite being sandwiched in a tiny tent between three men every night—one of whom happened to be Hambone, with his distinct pig odor—Tyvian found himself falling asleep the moment his head hit his blanket roll.

His efforts had two additional side effects. The first and less consequential one was that Hambone had now become his friend. He seemed to think getting his kneecap knocked askew with a small shovel was the best thing that ever happened to him. "Weren't for you," he said one night over the evening's share of mutton stew, "I wouldn't be riding the wagon. Be out there with you lot, marching my legs down to nothing."

"Just say the word," Tyvian said, "and I'll knock you on your arse again. Anytime."

Hambone had found this hilarious.

The second side effect was that Tyvian's time digging the latrine alone allowed him space to think over his predicament in private. While marching, he was too concerned with staying in rank and not dropping his pike (or Hambone's), but in the cool of the evening, alone with his stupid little shovel, Tyvian could take a deep breath and forget, for a moment, that his new name was Duchess and he was the unpaid foot soldier of Banric Sahand's invading army.

Like his sticking up for Hambone, Tyvian's plan to fake his own death had been a selfless act to its core—it had to be, since if it hadn't, he would have died as he plummeted off the roof of the Peregrine Palace into the lake below. As a selfless act, however, it had lacked a certain degree of postmortem planning. He had informed Eddereon to fish him out of the lake and hide him away until he recovered, but had also tasked him with finding a means by which they could leave the country unnoticed. This, he had to admit, Eddereon had done, albeit in the least pleasant way possible.

But now what?

Tyvian had no intention of remaining a member of the Ghouls for one moment longer than necessary. It was only a matter of time before orders from on high would put him (and Eddereon) in an untenable situation vis-à-vis the ring. As it stood, Tyvian knew full well that the mutton they were eating each night wasn't from any kind of elaborate baggage train—the Ghouls were stripping the countryside bare of every chicken, lamb, duck, and cow they could clap their gauntlets on. The villages they marched through locked their doors and shutters as they passed. Sometimes at dawn, Tyvian could see the oily columns of smoke rising to the sky—farms that had been burned by Captain Rodall's foraging teams the night before.

The idea that his mother was still alive and imprisoned in Dellor struck Tyvian as wildly improbable. Sahand was not known for his mercy and, even if his mother were alive, it was only because the torture she was enduring was so elaborate that she had not yet been permitted to expire. Running to Dellor—on foot, incidentally—would accomplish very little except put them in *Dellor*, which by all accounts was one of the least pleasant places in the West. No, Tyvian was not the one to rescue Lyrelle. The woman was on her own.

That fact, though, had yet to penetrate Eddereon's wooly brain. Late at night, while Hambone snored and their other tent-mate, a giant of a man by the name of Mort, evidently wrestled bears in his sleep, Eddereon and Tyvian would sometimes whisper to one another.

"You can't be serious about going to Dellor," Tyvian said one night, throwing Mort's huge hand off his face.

"She's in danger, Tyvian. She's your *mother*," Eddereon said, his eyes barely visible in the slash of moonlight that squeezed between their tent flaps.

"I'm telling you, as her *son*, that Lyrelle Reldamar has never wanted help from anybody, least of all me. If she wound up in Dellor, it's because she knew she would. That means she's either dead already, or well on her way to a triumphant escape. The last thing she needs is your schoolyard heroics."

"Tyvian." Eddereon reached out and grabbed his arm. "Don't you owe her this much?"

"*Owe* her? We're square, believe me." Tyvian yanked his arm free. "Besides, why do you care anyway? What do *you* owe her?"

Eddereon's eyes grew damp. He wiped away a tear with one filthy thumb. "Because, Tyvian—I *love* her."

So there it was. Lyrelle Reldamar had gotten her hooks so deep in Eddereon's idiot heart that he was about to cross a featureless wasteland and assail an impregnable fortress all in the hopes she wasn't skinned, stuffed, and adorning Banric Sahand's trophy case.

It was clear Eddereon could not be relied upon. That meant it would soon be time to ditch him, too.

If he was giving up the hero business, though, what else was there for Tyvian to do? He thought of one of his conversations with Xahlven—the Oracle of the Vale, he had said, knew how to find the Yldd. Find the Yldd and he could remove the ring. He could go back to being himself again—a new beginning, as it were. No more lowly moralistic concerns, no more requisite acts of heroic daring. He looked at the ring in the firelight one night over dinner. It was caked with grime, blackened by the day's efforts. Were it not for it, he would be dead. Of course, were it not for it, he would also never have found himself on that palace roof in the first place. There was so much he owed that trinket and so much it owed *him*, that it had become pointless to pass blame. Besides, he believed his mother when she had told him it was really just a storage unit for and amplifier of his better self. There was no sense arguing that, on some level, all the things he had done at the ring's coaxing were things he thought were right.

But that didn't mean he needed to keep it forever. Again, that feeling of freedom sought to overwhelm him. If he disappeared one night—if he crept off and got away—there was literally no limit to what he could do. No responsibilities, no debts, not even any enemies! Carlo diCarlo always said he knew how to get to the Vale—hell, if anybody knew something like that, it would be Carlo. All Tyvian needed to do was give the Ghouls the slip, get to Freegate, and then begin the next chapter in his life. The thought of kicking back in Carlo's house, a glass of *cherille* in his hand, while one of Carlo's girls rubbed the kinks from his back and the cramps from his legs . . . gods, it was enough to keep Tyvian going the whole next day with a smile on his face. Not even Drawsher's bawling could crack it.

Tyvian began to develop his plan for escape. The primary obstacle was Rodall's hounds—fooling hounds like that was nearly impossible without sorcerous intervention. At minimum, he was going to need about five gallons of human urine. Fortunately, he knew just where to get it—he had to dig the damned latrine every night. Even with all that piss, though, that would only buy him a half hour or so before they found the trail again. He set his mind to remembering his Eretherian geography—he'd smuggled things through this country so many times, he knew plenty of bolt holes and hideaways. He just needed a safe haven . . .

"Duchess!" Drawsher kicked him in the foot. For the barest second, Tyvian thought that maybe his plan to escape had been found out. But then he noticed Drawsher's expression—that unique kind of bitterness that arises when a bully has to admit they are wrong. "Captain is asking to see you. Hop to it."

Tyvian crawled out of the tent and stood, stretching his aching back. "What's this about?"

Drawsher pointed toward the command tent. "Don't keep the captain waiting, scrub! Move it!"

Tyvian walked toward the captain's tent with an easy gait. "What's the matter, Drawsher—weren't *you* invited?"

"Kroth take you, high-born shit-eating . . ." The sergeant made as though to chase him, fists balled, but something kept him at bay. Probably the fact that if Tyvian showed up to Rodall's tent late and with a black eye, Drawsher would be the one limping for the next week.

Tyvian savored the sergeant's impotence as he went to answer his employer's call. He felt so good at that moment, he even felt the desire to whistle coming on. Then he remembered exactly where he was going and his mood sobered. *After a week of marching and no word, what the hell could Rodall want now?*

Rodall's tent had no guards posted—just two of those enormous dogs curled up and sleeping on the mat before the door. Their heads popped up when Tyvian was five paces away and they watched carefully as he approached. One of them growled—a higher-pitched version of Hool's growl, but nevertheless pretty menacing. Tyvian stopped in his tracks.

Rodall whistled from inside the tent. "Let him in, boys."

Rodall was still wearing his armor—Tyvian was beginning to suspect the man slept in it. His tent featured a folding table with a huge map rolled up and lying across it. Tyvian didn't flatter himself to think that Rodall had hidden his company's exact location and disposition for *his* benefit. The captain was about to receive a visitor, then—a visitor he did not entirely trust.

Rodall looked at him and pointed to a weapons rack in the corner of the tent. "Get a sword and stand behind me. I want the weapon bared and point-down in the ground between your legs—don't say a damned thing, but keep your eyes open and be ready for anything, understand?"

Tyvian saluted. "Yes sir."

As Tyvian was doing as he was asked, Rodall caught him by the elbow and whispered in his ear. "If you breathe a word of anything you're about to hear to *anybody* . . ."

He let himself trail off, leaving the punishment to the imagination. Tyvian didn't have to imagine very hard.

Tyvian got to his "imposing bodyguard" position just in time to hear Rodall's hounds growl at a new visitor. Rodall drew a dagger from a scabbard and slipped it into his boot. Then he slid gently into a chair, the table between him and the door. He whistled his dogs off. "Come in."

A small woman stepped over the dogs and into the tent. She was dressed in a long black cloak, but Tyvian glimpsed a sword at her hip as she took in the tent. She reached up with gloved hands and gently pulled back her hood. Midnight curls, delicate features, blind in one eye . . .

It was Adatha Voth.

Kroth.

Tyvian froze. How many seconds before she recognized him? His heart pounded in his chest. His immediate instinct was to put his borrowed sword through the base of Rodall's skull while he had the chance and then see if he could cut his way out of the tent before Voth put a throwing knife in his spine. Of course, the ring would never permit him to do such a thing—stab a man in the back without cause—so while Tyvian was going through a secondary plan, he noticed something:

Voth had barely looked at him. She had noted his presence and the sword in his hands and the tabard on his chest, but that was it. The beard, the bald head, the poor nutrition and hard marching—Tyvian must not look remotely himself.

He was relieved, and yet . . . after all they'd shared, his pride was just a *touch* hurt.

Rodall eyed her warily, his hand resting on his

knee beneath the table, in easy reach of the dagger in his boot. "Sahand sent you?"

Voth watched Rodall with razor-sharp focus. Tyvian could tell she knew about the knife Rodall had in reach, and Tyvian discerned from some subtle movements that she had just let a small throwing knife drop into the palm of her hand. If Rodall saw this, he gave no sign. "I need to speak with you privately, Captain," she said.

"I might be a stupid old mercenary captain," Rodall said. "But I'm smart enough not to be alone with *you*, assassin."

Voth laughed—that throaty, sexy laugh Tyvian remembered so well from their evenings together in the House of Eddon, in a literally different life. "My dear captain—if I were sent here to kill you, do you really think you would have been told to expect me?"

Told? Told how? Tyvian hadn't spotted any couriers coming or going, nor any messenger djinn. He cast an eye around the room—there, in the corner, was a sending stone. Rodall must be in direct contact with his commanders, which meant he was in contact with Sahand. The risks of his discovery just got even more serious.

Meanwhile, the standoff between Voth and Rodall had not abated. With slow movements, Voth pulled open her cloak to reveal a scroll tube in a concealed pocket. She pulled it out and threw it on the table. "There. This ought to explain things. It seems I'm going to be tagging along with your little band of cannibals for the immediate future."

Rodall opened the scroll case. *Idiot*, Tyvian thought. *If Voth wanted him dead, there would have been a poison needle concealed in the lid.*

The captain glanced at the document, which was sealed with Sahand's personal mark in the wax. He looked over his shoulder. "You—leave us."

Tyvian didn't need to be asked twice. Part of him wanted to stick around and eavesdrop, but Rodall's hounds seemed disinclined toward his company. He decided to play it safe, even though with Voth in the camp he felt *decidedly* less safe.

What was Voth doing here? Could she . . . could she *know* or suspect he was alive? Could Sahand? Was Eddereon in danger? Should he warn him?

The ring throbbed in a dull, monotonous rhythm. *Dammit all.*

He turned back toward his tent. Desertion, it seemed, would have to wait for another day. He slipped back between his three tent-mates, marinating in their manly odors, and tried his best to get comfortable.

For the first time since he'd joined the Ghouls, Tyvian found he couldn't sleep.

CHAPTER 3

EARNING PAY

Tyvian spent the next few days waiting for the other shoe to drop. It never did. Rumors of Voth's arrival were rampant—Rodall's personal whore, some said. Others insisted she was a sorceress. Tyvian refused to offer an opinion. When someone asked what he thought, he'd say he didn't know either way. Voth? Who's that? Never heard of her.

In the meantime, Tyvian was getting a reputation for being the world's best mule. Even Drawsher seemed mutely appreciative of the fact that he'd been carrying Hambone's pack for days without falling behind a step. "That's what yer good for, Duchess," he said once, tapping Tyvian's shoulder with his rod. "Carrying baggage."

Tyvian couldn't help but snort. *If the man only knew . . .*

Hambone got back on his feet just in time for their first battle. Well, a skirmish, more like—Captain Rodall wasn't about to deploy his greenest troops against anything that resembled a dangerous foe. They were mustered into ranks early one morning without explanation and marched to a green outside a small village. There they stood, pikes high—a mute display of force—while Rodall "negotiated" with the village leaders.

Tyvian squinted across the grassy meadow at the motley assembly of peasants with pots on their heads who had dared to oppose them. A few of them had small hunting bows—the kind you used to kill ducks in a pond. The ring throbbed. *If it comes to fighting, this isn't going to be a skirmish. It's going to be murder.*

Captain Rodall, astride his coal-black charger with his hounds at his heels, had advanced twenty paces from the two blocks he'd tasked to this operation— one of pikes, the other of broadswords and shields. He had Drawsher on one side of him and Adatha Voth on the other, both of them also mounted. Despite what he'd heard in the tent, Tyvian had to assume that if Voth were with the Ghouls, she was here to murder someone. Given that Tyvian was not yet dead, he presumed that someone wasn't him.

He very much wanted to sneak out of his tent at night and find where in the camp she was bedded down. He wanted to lurk outside the command tent and eavesdrop on her discussions with Rodall. Of course, he was not alone—the presence of a beautiful woman in the camp was enough to drive half the Ghouls to distraction. Serving as her "escort" in camp had become a coveted position, afforded only those with the longest service records with the company— and "Duchess" didn't rate. Besides, the closer he got, the more likely she'd recognize him, and he had been lucky enough the first time around to dissuade him from trying his luck for a second go.

"Duchess," Hambone nudged him, "what're they saying? We gonna fight?"

Tyvian tore his attention from Voth's black curls. "What?"

"C'mon—do the trick!" Hambone thrust his chin toward the captain's delegation and the three villagers who had come out to meet him.

Mort spat a wad of chewing tobacco into the grass. "What trick?"

Hambone giggled. "Duchess can read lips!"

Mort looked down at Tyvian. Standing nearly taller than Hool, this was a long way down for Mort. Tyvian felt like an ant. "The hell he can!"

"I certainly can, and if you two would shut up, I will." Tyvian adjusted his helm to get the best view. Hambone and Mort fell silent, and he felt the rank behind him leaning in to listen to whatever he was going to say. "I can't see the captain's mouth, so I don't know what he's saying, but I can see the villagers well enough."

Silence for a moment as Tyvian parsed out the words. "Well?" Hambone whispered.

"The fellow's making Rodall an offer. They'll give us a dozen chickens and five pigs in exchange for us marching away."

Mort snorted through his cavernous nostrils. "We're just gonna kill 'em and take 'em anyway."

"But if we just take that much, we can march away and none of us get killed."

Mort spat again. "Them farmers ain't enough to kill me—won't kill nobody in this company. Captain knows it, too. You'll see."

Hambone was grinning. "And then we get paid!"

Tyvian glimpsed nods from the corner of his eye. The Ghouls were excited, especially the bones. If they got to stick their pikes into some peasants today, they'd be eligible for the Ghouls' very generous salary of three silver crowns a week. The ring tightened on Tyvian's finger to the point that it went numb. *And what do you propose I do about it?* Tyvian thought.

He felt a hand on his back—Eddereon, standing right behind him. The big man whispered in Tyvian's ear. "This is going to get ugly. Prepare yourself."

Tyvian nodded, though he had no realistic idea

of what "preparing himself" would look like in this scenario.

The villagers' delegation had finished talking. Tyvian supposed this was the point when Captain Rodall would tell the head villager in which end to stuff his bribe. Before he started speaking, though, Drawsher wheeled his horse and rode back toward the pikes. *Here we go . . .*

Rodall drew his broadsword and cut down the head villager with a savage blow to the temple that took the top of the man's head off. On the backswing, he cut the arm off the lanky boy who was holding the village "standard"—just a plain blue flag on a stick. The third person—an old woman—screamed and fled, clutching her skirts. The captain twitched a finger, and his hounds leapt after her, running her down with ease. Her screams as they tore her apart made the ring blaze to the point that Tyvian's knees felt weak. He leaned on his pike.

Rodall and Voth wheeled their horses and headed back toward the Ghouls. A few arrows struck Rodall's bow wards and bounced off. Voth was laughing.

Tyvian glanced back to see Eddereon clutching his right hand to his chest. Tyvian knew that exact feeling—the ring torturing him. Tyvian felt it too, from a numbing squeeze to a red-hot fire. An iron brand laid across his fingers and blazing up his forearm.

The drums sounded the advance.

Tyvian had little choice but to match pace with

the pike block, but his feet were so heavy he felt like he was wading through mud. Beside him, he heard Hambone say, "Here we go!"

The peasants—about fifty of them—ranged from boys of maybe thirteen to old men two steps from the grave. It was probably the entire male population of the village here. They were armed with hatchets and pitchforks and scythes and other tools of agriculture and husbandry. They had pot lids and barrel tops for shields. He hadn't been seeing things, either—they truly wore iron cooking pots on their heads.

They were screaming with rage.

Some old fellow with an actual rusty sabre—a makeshift sergeant—thrust his blade toward the approaching pike block. Arrows from the back rank of the village militia whistled in low arcs. They mostly missed, but a few managed to plink off the Ghouls' helmets. Tyvian heard one man cry out—probably hit in the leg or arm. The drums doubled their pace, and so did the Ghouls. Tyvian lowered his pike. Over his shoulders, the pikes of the ranks behind him lowered as well. The twenty-five-man block was a solid wall of steel spikes, moving toward the peasants at an even march. The other block—the sword block—was wheeling wide. When the pikes engaged, the swords would sweep down on those villagers seeking to flee. Tyvian could only glance at the other unit between the waving weapon shafts that surrounded him, but he knew what was going on. It was obvious, really. Inevitable.

Half of the peasants charged, throwing themselves at the mercenaries, sledgehammers and wood splitters held high. The other half broke and ran.

It was hard to say who had the worst of it.

The first villager to come within range of Tyvian's pike was a boy—a big barrel-chested lad, a bit like Hambone. He had a pitchfork. The ring atrophied Tyvian's arms—he couldn't do anything. He couldn't stab the boy, but of course he didn't have to. Hambone did, as did the pikeman just behind him and to his left, spitting the farmboy through the chest in two places. In a dying spasm, he threw his pitchfork at the block. It plinked off of Tyvian's mail; it would probably leave a bruise. But then they were marching over the dying boy, their weapons poking holes in the next villager and the next and the next.

Tears streaked Tyvian's cheeks as the fire in his hand burned. It was all he could do to hold the pike, but it hung down at his waist, inert—just a long pole to ward off danger. Five other peasants went down under the foot-long tips of the Ghouls' weapons. Then the order came to drop the pikes and the formation broke up. Swords were drawn. The villagers were routed, and now the slaughter was set to begin.

Hambone whooped, waving his sword in the air, and charged into the fray. Mort was more deliberate, carefully stabbing injured villagers in the spine before advancing.

Tyvian let them go. He supposed he ought to be screaming at himself to get over it—to do something before someone noticed and his cover was blown. He supposed also he ought to have been angry at the idiot peasants who thought threatening a mercenary company with a couple of old men with garden tools was a wise plan. But he remembered, at alternate points in his life, thinking and doing just those kinds of things.

Not now, however. Not today. He could still remember the faces of all those people who had come to his coronation. The ones that had kissed his hands and wept with joy at the very sight of him. The ones that, ultimately, he'd thrown himself off a building to save.

And a fat lot of good that had done.

Somebody smacked him in the back of the head. It was Drawsher—on foot, his eyes wild. "Get your head out your arse, Duchess! Earn your pay!"

Tyvian nodded, his hand still blazing with pain, and dropped his pike. He followed Drawsher as he charged through the village and into a pigsty. The sergeant spitted a young pig with a precise thrust and then passed the corpse to Tyvian. "Hold that! That there's mine, understand? For later."

A woman in a bonnet poked her head out of a doorway and shot an arrow at Drawsher. It stuck in his mail, just below the collarbone, but the bow just wasn't strong enough to pierce deep. Drawsher staggered back a pace, roaring. Then he charged into the house.

Tyvian, still holding the bleeding pig, followed him. He could scarcely think—the pain was so intense. It had never been this bad before. The world was just a tunnel of fire and blood, and at the end was Drawsher's broad back, pieces of his kit jingling as he ran.

They were in the cottage. The woman was screaming, throwing pots and plates and bowls at Drawsher as she sought to keep the butcher's table between her and the sergeant. Drawsher batted the projectiles aside with his shield and leered. "Only gonna make it all the sweeter, duckling! I like the fighters!"

Tyvian dropped the dead pig.

Drawsher glared at him. "Go search the rest of the house, bone!"

Tyvian drew his sword. "No."

Getting through Drawsher's guard took only two moves. Tyvian left his broadsword sticking in the sergeant's eye, its tip pushing through the back of Drawsher's skull and his chain coif and pinning him to a wooden support beam.

The pain torturing him subsided, if momentarily. The woman screamed and fled. *Not even a thank you.* But his next thought was this: *What does she have to krothing thank you for, anyway?*

Numb, Tyvian worked his sword out of Drawsher's

face. He had to put his foot on the man's breastbone to get it out.

Outside there was a flash of fire, and a wave of heat rushed through the open door. Tyvian went outside to see three Ghouls lying on their backs, their bodies smoking. Across the village square, on the roof of what was probably a blacksmith's shop, an old woman was waving around a wand. *A hedge wizard.*

She fired another ball of flame at some more men, but these were a bit more nimble and dove behind a water trough. One of them was Hambone. His face was blistering up from a severe burn. He was screaming.

The hedge wizard powered up her wand again and shot another fireball at a group of the sword block that was trying to advance on the smithy. They scattered.

From the ground floor of the smithy, three men with bows started shooting. With the wizard's wand providing cover, they could take their time and aim well. Two more Ghouls went down.

What the hell do I do now?

"Duchess!" It was Hambone, screaming to him from behind his trough. "Get that bitch on the roof! Get her!"

Tyvian looked down. There was a bow at his feet—the woman's bow.

Tyvian had never shot a bow in his entire life.

A fireball exploded against the trough, causing it

to light on fire. The men hunkered down with Hambone, screaming.

The ring sent Tyvian conflicting signals. On the one hand, the Ghouls had already lit half the village aflame and killed dozens of people. On the other, that old woman with the wand was trying to kill his ostensible friends. His whole right arm tingled with the conflict. He froze up.

In the end, he didn't have to decide. The hedge wizard dropped her wand and clawed at her neck. Behind her, gloved hands twisted a garrote deeper into the old woman's throat.

Of course, it was Adatha Voth.

CHAPTER 4

THE SPOILS

Tyvian spent the remainder of the "battle" in a pain-soaked stupor. The ring inflicted on him every torture, every hurt, and every death the Ghouls perpetrated. He knew he might have picked up a sword and begun a campaign of violence on his own, but to what end? Nothing could save that nameless little village now, least of all him. He might have felt the satisfaction of cutting the throats of a half-dozen rapists and murderers, but that scenario only ended with him running through the fields from Captain Rodall and his dogs, hunting new ears for his necklace.

So he curled himself into a ball somewhere, closed his eyes, and waited for it all to be over. Like a stinking coward. He only wondered, as he listened to the screams of the women and the crying children, how Eddereon was faring in all this. No better, certainly. Or perhaps Eddereon's better self wasn't quite as good as his own.

When it had quieted down some, the horn was sounded for retreat. Tyvian crawled out from beneath the oxcart he'd been hiding under and tried to leave the village without looking at anything. The heat from the burning homes hit him in waves. He had to step over a little boy—perhaps five years old—whose head was bashed open like a melon. One of his tiny, shoeless feet still twitched. The ring burned Tyvian from within while real flames burned him from without. He felt like his bones were grinding together, dry and brittle as sandpaper. He gasped, trying to keep the tears from falling. Somehow, he pressed on.

Back on the meadow where the village's fallen defenders lay, the pain subsided somewhat. Tyvian managed an erect posture; he could look around. On either side of him he saw his tent-mates. Mort had a goat over his broad shoulders, his boots caked in blood. Despite the burns on his face, Hambone was laughing with another man. "Shoulda heard her squeal, mate! Gods, what a ride that was!"

Tyvian threw up.

This caught their attention. "Well, well," Hambone said with a snort, "if it ain't Duchess! Where were you hiding, eh? Missed all the fun!"

Still leaning on his knees, Tyvian spat and struggled to catch his breath. "Yes . . . my . . . my loss . . ."

Hambone laughed at him. "Seems like there's something I do better'n you, after all. Ain't there, Duchess?"

Tyvian couldn't help but choke out a laugh. "Yes . . . seems so."

They were mustered into loose ranks. The lack of Sergeant Drawsher was noticed immediately. Captain Rodall summoned a few of the senior Ghouls— Eddereon included in this—and sent them back to the village to fetch him. Tyvian knew this was bad, but was too wrung out to care. There were few tortures a bunch of Delloran thugs could devise that he had not just experienced tenfold. Having his ears cut off sounded like a refreshing change of pace.

Eddereon and the others came back after a brief search, Drawsher's body draped between them. The men stared. "Kroth's teeth," Hambone said, eyes wide, "who coulda taken Drawsher? He was a beast! An utter beast!"

"Maybe he owed somebody money, eh?" Mort was stroking the goat's head to keep it from bleating. Now that Tyvian could see him from the front, he could tell where the blood all over his boots came from— from his belt hung five headless chickens.

Hambone's eyes shot up. "You think . . . one of *us* did that?"

Mort shrugged, refusing to comment.

Eddereon and the other men carried the body

away. The rest of them were ordered to form into a column and marched back to camp a mile or so distant. The mood, though initially jubilant, had soured notably. The men seemed downtrodden, heads hanging as they carried along their stolen chickens, pigs, and goats, the smoke from the burning village still thick in the air.

Tyvian wanted to scream at them all. *Seriously? You just raped and murdered a bunch of unarmed farmers and you're depressed because the man who beat you with a switch every morning got stabbed through the skull?*

But, as he had the past number of days, he said nothing.

He hated his own silence.

With every step away from the village, the ring's anger eased somewhat, though not entirely. It was there constantly, pushing him toward either justice or vengeance, though at this point Tyvian could not readily tell the difference between the two.

Back at camp, the stolen provisions were confiscated by the company quartermaster and recorded in a massive iron-bound ledger. Each man was searched by a pair of burly sell-swords with hands the size of ham hocks—the process had more in common with a beating than anything else. Men were permitted to keep money and trinkets and such, but food and drink was dropped into labeled barrels. Altogether, the razing of a pastoral Eretherian village was extremely organized.

When it came to be Tyvian's turn, the men turned

up nothing. The quartermaster, who had gold-rimmed spectacles clipped to a long, booze-rotted nose, actually looked up from his ledger. "Nothing?"

Tyvian shrugged. "Nothing I wanted."

Everyone looked at him like he'd just pulled off his own head and tried to bowl with it. The quartermaster blinked, his eyes magnified by his spectacles. "You know that these provisions are important for the company's survival, yes?"

"I'm very sorry for not doing my part," Tyvian droned. "Um . . . sir."

The magnified eyes of the quartermaster narrowed. "What is your name?"

"Duchess."

"Your *real* name?"

"Ty . . . ahhh . . . blast it . . . Arick of . . . somewhere."

If the fact that Tyvian didn't remember his own name raised any suspicions, the quartermaster gave no sign—Tyvian imagined people joined mercenary companies under false names all the time anyway. The man scribbled a note and waved him off. Tyvian went back to his tent and waited for his comeuppance to arrive.

It came at sundown. Tyvian's whole block was mustered. Captain Rodall was there, hands resting on the pommel of his broadsword, which was currently stuck point-first in the ground. Beside him was Voth, who was sitting on a large rock and cleaning under her fingernails with a stiletto.

Eddereon had evidently been given a field promotion to sergeant—the benefits of being a legendary mercenary, Tyvian supposed. After Eddereon had inspected his unit and noted that all men were present, saving those few wounded in the action that day, he took his place at Rodall's right hand. The captain nodded at his new sergeant and then flashed a silvery smile at the men. "Sergeant Drawsher was killed by a broadsword to the eye. One thrust, quick and hard—right through the back of his skull." Drawsher nodded, scanning them, one by one. "No Eretherian pig's boy or grandpa did this. It was one of our own."

Tyvian felt the tension in the unit ramp up. He could tell that men were holding their breath, that others were tensing for what was to come next. He didn't do anything, though. With Voth sitting there, looking at the men, anything to distinguish himself from the crowd might be a death sentence in more ways than one.

Rodall was still talking. "We can't stay here long. We march tonight, so we're going to settle this quick. The man who killed Drawsher can step forward now, and we'll have it done with quick and painless. If he doesn't, well . . ." Rodall's silver grin sparkled in the fading sunlight. "I just kill two of you at random and call it even. If the rest of you find out who done it later and take things into your own hands, can't say I'd mind that, either."

Silence. Tyvian clenched his teeth. Had anyone seen him? Would someone turn him in?

Rodall walked down the line, sword over one shoulder. "Can't say as I blame a man who'd put steel through Drawsher. He was a certain kind of son of a bitch, for sure. He was a cheap death, too—no children, no wife. No death pay for me to spend, eh?"

Tyvian held his breath as Voth's gaze passed over him and paused, just for a moment, before moving on. The ring was beginning to throw fits again, squeezing and burning and pinching. It wasn't about to let two others die for his deed. *Dammit, dammit, dammit!*

Rodall stopped two-thirds through the line and pointed his blade at one of the younger bones—Tyvian didn't remember his name, just the size of his ears and his creaky voice. "You. Step forward."

The boy fell to his knees. "Oh, please, Captain sir, I didn't do it! I swear, I—"

Rodall thrust his sword down through the boy's open mouth and into his chest cavity. Blood fountained up and the lad's arms and legs twitched for a moment, then he was still. Rodall put his foot in the boy's chest and pulled the sword free. The body tumbled backward, his legs pinned beneath him. The men nearby stepped back.

The ring made Tyvian wince so hard he actually cried out. He closed his eyes, trying to swallow the pain somehow. There was no escape.

Rodall stepped in front of him. "Something you want to confess, Duchess?"

Tyvian clenched his teeth. "N . . . no."

Rodall snickered. "Step forward, then."

"Begging your pardon, sir!" Hambone broke in, his voice quavering. "But . . . but Duchess didn't kill nobody, sir! He . . . he couldn't have—he spent the whole battle curled up like a baby! Like . . . like a little girl, sir!"

Tyvian looked at the stocky Delloran pig farmer with openmouthed shock. "Hambone, shut the hell up!"

Rodall turned toward Hambone. "Would you like to take his place, bone?"

Hambone was pale. "W-With respect . . . s-sir . . . I ain't no bone no more. Blooded today, see?"

Rodall laughed and looked back at Eddereon. "You were right, Ed! These boys have spunk, don't they? Ha!" He looked back at Hambone and the smile dropped from his face. "Step forward and on your knees, *bone*."

Hambone gulped. "I . . . I . . ."

Rodall pointed to the grass. "Knees!"

Hambone looked at Tyvian, his eyes wide, mouth hanging open—he looked like a man about to drown. He stepped forward on wooden legs. He slowly sank to his knees.

Dammit all! Tyvian stepped between Hambone and Rodall. "It's me! I did it. I killed Drawsher!"

Hambone looked poleaxed. "Wh . . . what? You did no such thing! Duchess, don't be stupid!"

"Hambone, you insufferable dunce, between the two of us, the stupid one is *always you!*"

Rodall laughed, his platinum-capped teeth flashing. He motioned Hambone up with the tip of his sword. "Back in ranks!" He pointed to a spot on the grass a bit in front of the line of men—somewhere they all could see. "Kneel over there, Duchess. And be a man about it this time."

Eddereon stepped forward, "Sir, if I might—"

"Shut it, Ed," Rodall snarled. "This little priss cost me two men now. I'm going to get back my money's worth."

Tyvian walked forward. The ring, for the first time in hours, fell silent. He wondered to himself if its resurrection powers extended to decapitations. He decided he just wasn't that lucky. He got to the spot indicated and knelt. Voth was looking right at him, her good eye squinting, her head cocked.

What the hell. Tyvian winked at her.

Rodall's armored boots clanked up behind him. "You know I lied about the painless thing, right?"

Tyvian spoke over his shoulder. "My mother always told me not to trust a Ghoul."

Rodall kicked him hard in the kidneys. Tyvian gasped and fell on his face. The tip of Rodall's sword, still slick with the blood of its last kill, pressed between Tyvian's thighs and slid, slowly, toward the crease of his buttocks. Tyvian clenched—this . . . this was going to hurt. A lot.

"Rodall!" Voth shouted. "I pick him."

The captain's sword paused. "What?"

"I have my pick of men—I pick *him*. Don't damage him."

Rodall's sword didn't waver. "This is a discipline issue, Adatha! I settle it *my* way!"

Voth hopped down off her rock and walked right up to the captain. "And when I report back to the prince and tell him you weren't entirely cooperative with me, how do you suppose he will react?" She pointed at Tyvian. "Do you think he might have to settle a 'discipline issue' of his own?"

"Are you *threatening* me? In front of my own men?"

Voth chuckled. "Don't bother, Rodall—I'm not a girl who gives an arse about your problems. I'm a representative of your damned employer, and you *do what I say*."

Tyvian lay on his face in the grass for another few moments, the feeling of a broadsword between his thighs. Then, finally, it was withdrawn. "Take him, then, but keep him out of my sight, understand? I'd hate there to be an *accident*."

Voth grinned up at the armored sell-sword captain and faked a curtsey. "Accidents can happen to quite a lot of people, Rodall. *Especially* when I'm around."

Tyvian rolled over and got a look at Rodall's face. It was positively feral with anger—Tyvian had seen raccoons trapped in barrels who'd looked happier. He roared at the block of soldiers, "Dismissed!" Then, spitting on Tyvian's chest, he stormed away.

Tyvian staggered to his feet. Voth was there, helping him up. Her lips were close to his ear: "Well, well, well—aren't *you* full of surprises, *Tyvian*."

Voth's tent was a palace compared to the canvas doghouse Tyvian had slept in for the last two weeks. It was lit by a brass feylamp dangling from a chain. Thick Kalsaari rugs carpeted the ground; a circular bed with silk sheets occupied much of the available space. No sooner had they entered than Voth threw Tyvian on it and pounced on him.

Tyvian had been expecting to be murdered or, if not that, at least yelled at. Instead, he found Voth kissing him with the kind of reckless passion usually reserved by starving men for bread. She had her arms locked around his neck, her legs straddling his waist, and her lips so firmly sealed around his own that Tyvian couldn't have escaped if he wanted to.

As it happened, he rapidly discovered that he *didn't* want to. He let her midnight curls surround his face, soft and smelling of fresh leather, and put one hand on her back, pulling her close. She moaned appreciatively and kissed him hard. With that encouragement, Tyvian threw caution to the wind and put his other hand firmly on her arse.

Voth broke the kiss. "Take off your clothes."

"Isn't there . . . well . . . shouldn't we talk about—"

"No." Voth pulled open her vest and shirt with a savage tug. She was wearing nothing underneath. "Strip. Now."

Tyvian did as he was told. He did not regret it.

Outside the tent, in the camp around them, Tyvian heard a lot of commotion—they were breaking camp, getting ready to move. In Voth's arms, however, the world outside seemed distant, unimportant. It was like another life—some kind of nightmare he'd woken up from.

When they had finished their lovemaking—if that was the proper word for something that left that many scratches on his back—Voth rose from the bed and got dressed immediately. She wasn't a cuddler, apparently. He also noted that the singular piece of clothing she *was* still wearing—and had been during the entire amorous episode—was a slender stiletto sheath strapped to her calf. He couldn't help but smile at her.

She tossed his hose at him. "Get dressed. We've got to get packed up or they'll leave us behind."

Tyvian motioned to the bed. "Are we going to talk about what the hell just happened here?"

Voth smiled at him. "It was good, Reldamar—is that what you need? I've never enjoyed a dirtier man. There—get up." She began throwing things into a large chest.

Tyvian got up, pulled on his hose, and started

hunting around for his shirt. "Not that—though compliments are always appreciated. I mean . . . well . . . do I even need to ask?"

Voth rolled her good eye. "Fine, fine—I was paid to kill you. That didn't mean I didn't find you attractive. Now that you are dead and my former employer is dead, there is absolutely nothing stopping me from having my way with you, and I intend to do so whenever I feel like it. Is that satisfactory?"

Velia Hesswyn is dead? Tyvian pushed the surprise away in favor of more pressing concerns. "What's to stop you from turning me in to Sahand?"

"Absolutely nothing, and I'm so glad you understand our relationship at this point." Voth banged the lid of the trunk closed. "You're mine, Tyvian Reldamar. I have you by the balls in several different ways, and not all of them unpleasant for you."

There's always a catch. "All right, so besides my occasional *romantic* attentions, what exactly do you need me for?" Tyvian pulled on his shirt.

Voth was belting on a Galaspin sword—a kind of shorter, heavier rapier or narrower broadsword. "That is need-to-know information, and you do not yet need to know." She waved him outside. "Now get out and get ready to carry my things."

CHAPTER 5

BETWEEN THE LIVING AND THE DEAD

The mudlark, filthy and toothless, pulled the canvas off the dead bodies like an artist unveiling his life's work. He bowed low and gestured to the stinking, rotten corpses with fingerless gloves. "For inspection, Your Highness . . ."

Artus wrinkled his nose at the smell, but didn't retch—he'd seen enough rotting flesh in the past week to get past that particular affliction. Michelle had prepared him an enchanted handkerchief that would protect him from the stench—he had it in his sleeve now—but he refused to use it. Everybody might think him a prince, but he'd be damned if he behaved like one. Bad enough he was receiving guests in the ruins of the Peregrine Palace with a pair of undead bodyguards—the White Guard—flanking him.

Artus crouched in front of the closest body. Like all the others, it had been dragged from the bottom of Lake Elren, where it had probably been rotting since the Battle of Eretheria City two weeks prior. It was hard to tell what this man had looked like in life; scavengers from the lake bed, probably freshwater crabs and various fish, had eaten away much of the man's face. The pallid flesh was caked in black mud from head to toe. The clothing had been of fine quality, but now it was practically impossible to tell the color or precise style. Artus looked anyway, seeking identifiable characteristics—none.

The mudlark twiddled his fingers in anticipation. "You can see, Your Highness, this one's the right size, the proper height. Hair seems like it was red, yes?"

Artus grabbed the corpse's right arm and looked closely at the worm-eaten fingers. They were bare. "Not this one."

The mudlark hid his disappointment well. "It was but a guess, Your Highness, of course, of course. But *this* one," he motioned toward the second body, "this one was found with quite a lot of valuable magecraft on his person."

Artus shifted his attention to the other body, which was, if anything, in worse condition than the first. This one appeared to have caught on fire before plunging into the lake, given the state of the skull. "Do you *have* any of that magecraft?"

The mudlark smiled his toothless smile and bowed. "I'm afraid I weren't the first to the body, Your Highness. Other . . . what's the word—other *entrepreneurs* got there first."

In other words, the body had already been rifled over and anything valuable pawned. There was a whole industry of secondhand luxury sales that had sprung up almost overnight in Eretheria. A fellow who walked down North Street in Westercity could buy the heirlooms of at least twenty different noble lines off a cart for short money and pawn them again in Saldor or Ihyn for five times what was paid. Artus had seen survivors of the palace massacre—the lucky ones—clutching their signet rings and going through the boxes of discarded golden earrings and jeweled brooches, hoping to find signs of their loved ones' fates.

He had wandered there himself in the days following the battle, walking up and down the rows of little pawnshops, trying to pick out something that had belonged to Tyvian in a window somewhere. It was impossible—he had no idea what Tyvian had been wearing that night, and so he had no idea what might be there. Tyvian's collection of jewelry was comprehensive, after all. The only thing Artus *knew* Tyvian was wearing that night was not the kind of thing that would show up in a pawn shop window.

So he had to resort to more *direct* means.

"Do you know what was taken?" he asked the mudlark, trying to look the man in the eyes.

The mudlark bowed rather than meet his gaze. "Some wards enchanted in some brooches, I think, and three rings, all silver. He might've also had a blade, or maybe just a scabbard—I didn't get a good look, more's the pity."

Artus picked up the right hand of the corpse. There, nestled on the ring finger, was a plain iron band. His breath caught. *No.*

The mudlark smiled. "Your Highness sees it, eh? I knew it! I knew it! I told my brother and he didn't believe me—looking for something on the right hand, I tells him, and maybe a ring. And there it is!"

Artus thrust at finger at man. "Watch it with the big smiles, friend. This was . . . might have been . . ." He couldn't quite finish the sentence for the tears that sought to choke him.

The color drained from the mudlark's already pale face. He bowed deeply. "Oh! My apologies, Your Highness! I was forgetting myself! Of course, of course!"

The stink of rot nearly made Artus gag again. Clenching his teeth, he grabbed the ring and worried it off the corpse's finger. A fair amount of dead flesh came with it. *Damned thing* still *doesn't wanna come off.*

The ring was lighter than Artus had expected. He brushed away the filth and death until he could see it clearly. He produced Michelle's enchanted handkerchief and rubbed it clean.

The mudlark was still bowing. "I will not trouble Your Highness in his time of grief. If all's in order, I'll just collect my reward and—"

"Wait!" Artus held up a hand. The mudlark froze as the two White Guards silently stepped forward, their ivory *volto* masks peaceful as always.

Artus held the ring up to a shaft of sunlight pouring in from a hole in the distant palace roof. There, etched on the exterior of the ring in his hands, was the inscription A.V.B. WITH LOVE. Artus threw it on the floor. "That isn't the right ring."

The mudlark did not rise from his bow, but he did shuffle backward. The White Guards matched him, pace for pace. "Please, Your Highness—a mistake, is all. A misunderstanding!"

Artus found himself shouting. "You tried to trick me! You wanted to dupe me into thinking this was the king's body!"

The White Guards loomed over the mudlark, their long spears gleaming, their white robes perfectly still. The toothless, filthy man trembled beneath their nongaze. "No! I swear! Please, Your Highness! Mercy!"

Artus's heart pounded in his chest. He knew he had only to give the order and the undead constructs would kill this man instantly, without hesitation. There would be no repercussions, either—he was the Young Prince, beloved by the people, fresh back from his first victory in battle. He *wanted* to do it, too—this disgusting scavenger, looting dead bodies to sell their things to weeping widows and haggard old knights. The last two weeks had been nothing but death and blood and grief, and there were always men like this—grinning, soulless husks—making a few coppers off it. It made him more ill than the stench of any dozen corpses.

The mudlark had his face pressed to the floor, his whole body trembling. Artus took a deep breath. "Get out of here."

The mudlark cocked his head. "Wh . . . what? Truly?"

Artus turned away and waved him toward the door. "Just go. Don't come back."

The mudlark stood slowly, eyeing the stone-still White Guards still flanking him, and gave Artus a cautious salute. "You're a good man, Your Highness. A good man, blessed by Hann."

"Vanish already."

The mudlark left at a dead run. When he was gone, the two White Guards silently retook their places behind each of Artus's shoulders. He looked at them both, not for the first time wondering who or what they had been in life. Myreon had spread the word that they were Eretherian peasant levies killed in the spring campaigns of years past and buried in mass graves outside the city. Artus wasn't so sure. Though you couldn't see what they looked like, thanks to the masks and the white robes, Artus was pretty sure some of them were too short and too small to have ever been men-at-arms. He had, however, resisted the urge to unmask any of them. In the end, he just didn't want to know.

"Artus? Are you in here?" Artus turned to see Michelle entering through a servants' entrance at the far end of the hall, her gown of bright green flowing like a cloud behind her slender silhouette.

"Over here!" He waved. And then she was there, draping her thin arms around his neck and planting a soft kiss on his cheek. The feeling of her lips made his spine tingle.

"You were missed at the celebration! Everyone's asking for you." She looked down at the two bodies lying on the floor. Her face fell. "Oh Artus, why do you do this to yourself?"

Artus leaned his forehead against hers. "Do what?"

"The mudlarks. You dragging every person with a pulse in here to ask them about red-haired men. You're torturing yourself."

Artus placed a hand on his chest, feeling Tyvian's letter in the pocket where it always rested. "He's alive, Michelle. I know he's alive."

Michelle sighed and gave him another kiss, this one on the temple. "I know, my love. But if he is, then he wished to appear dead, and from what you've told me of him, he probably did it for a good reason."

Artus frowned. "No. He was just . . . just running away again." The words hurt to say, like a knot in his chest he couldn't remove. They always were followed by an unspoken phrase, one that echoed in Artus's mind as loud as thunder: *Except this time he didn't take me with him.*

Michelle seemed to sense his tension. Her delicate hands played with his hair. She pulled him close. "You've got to stop this, Artus. People are beginning to talk. They say you're mad with grief."

"Well, maybe I am." Artus pulled away from her. He found himself staring in a full-length mirror hanging on the wall. He was almost six feet tall now, with broad shoulders that supported a cape of royal blue linen clasped with gold at his throat. A shirt of enchanted mail, a mageglass broadsword, riding boots of fine Eddonish leather. Sandy blond hair that fell in ringlets just below his ears, a close-short goatee that was filling in nicely for once. Artus had trouble reconciling the man in the mirror with the street urchin who had once been in his place. The one who'd stuck with Tyvian Reldamar through a hundred adventures, only now to be alone.

Gods, he thought, *even Brana . . .*

Michelle came next to him, and wrapped her arms around his waist, and put her head on his shoulder. He felt some of the tension bleed out of him—Michelle always had that power, it seemed. She was so thin, Artus felt as though he could break her with one hand, and yet she'd become a kind of anchor for him. Without Hool and without Tyvian, Artus felt adrift for the first time in years. Even Brana would have offered a companion in disorientation. But instead of a gnoll-brother to wrestle with, now he had responsibilities, *expectations*—he was the Young Prince of Eretheria. Without Michelle there to hold him, he thought he might have gone mad.

Michelle gave him a squeeze. "You have duties to attend to, my prince."

Artus's stomach fell at the sound of those words—*my prince*. "Right. Sure—of course."

"You'll be a great leader, Artus. I know it. You just have to believe in yourself."

Artus didn't answer—he had no idea what was appropriate to say and didn't want to argue. It never felt right, arguing with Michelle, so he just let the young noblewoman hang on his arm as they walked out of the hall.

Outside, on the muddy ground of Peregrine Palace's once beautiful gardens, a great celebration was underway. Casks of beer, stacked in a pyramid, were tapped one after another to serve endless rows of peasant men in bleached white tabards—the soldiers of Myreon's new army. These men were the guests of honor, and a whirling carnival of musicians and dancers and games of chance had been erected to celebrate their victory. *His* victory.

Someone in the crowd recognized him. Beer tankards were raised and a thunderous cry of HUZZAH, THE PRINCE echoed off the scorched walls of the palace. They also saluted Michelle, who waved happily to the half-drunken, gleeful mob. Artus found himself searching their faces for his friends, all dead or gone. *Brana would have loved a party like this.*

"Go on," Michelle whispered into his ear. "Wave to your people."

They aren't my people. But Artus waved anyway. He smiled. He let himself be led across the gardens to the opposite wing of the palace. They might have arrived there without ever going outside, but Artus guessed Michelle wanted to be seen with him. She was staking her claim, as it were.

It was presumed by the world at large, if silently, that he and Michelle were to be married. They had not discussed this expectation themselves, though— there was something . . . delicate between them, Artus knew. Like dew on a spiderweb, he feared poking at it too much might ruin something forever. He could not tell how much of their relationship was based on . . . well . . . on him being a prince. Which he wasn't, no matter what Michelle said. But, at the same time, he was in no rush to dissuade her from thinking he was.

Artus had a hard time verbalizing such feelings. This little slip of a highborn girl, with her sharp features and her soft voice, seemed able to drive him mad with a gesture. He had not ever been in love—he hadn't ever thought he'd be that lucky—and now that he might be, he found himself full of doubts. Did she feel the same way? Was she using him? What if he wasn't *really* in love? What if he was stringing her along, only to ruin her later? The thought of making her cry was agony. The thought of his promise on that hellish night in the palace—that he would never let her go—haunted him. Who was he to take such an oath?

But, for all of that, when Michelle held him, when she laughed at his jokes, when her eyes shone with admiration of him—as they often did—he felt a warm glow deep inside, powering him forward. His heart rose into his throat at the thought of her smile or the feeling of her lips against his, and he knew that he would be a prince if he had to, if that meant he would have her. He suspected, though he didn't know, that this *was* love.

But he had no one to ask.

The prisoner—the leader of the now-defunct Army of Davram—was located in the least damaged wing of the palace. It was in this wing that most of the administrative "staff" for Myreon's burgeoning White Army was based, and so he and Michelle had to pass by rows of burly guild types—blacksmiths, carpenters, stonemasons, and the like—who had come to comprise most of Myreon's officer corps, in order to reach their rooms. They also cheered as Artus passed and doffed their hats to Michelle, smiling their gap-toothed and gold-capped smiles. Michelle elbowed him and told him to wave, so he waved.

These men were like a different species when compared to the kind of people who used to loiter about the Peregrine Palace. They were loud and poorly dressed, they laughed too long and smoked pipes indoors, but they had the unique distinction of being respected community leaders *without* being of noble birth. Loyalty to guild—a network of masters and journeymen and apprentices that stretched across the whole of Eretheria—was the foundation upon which Myreon was building her revolution.

But not a one of them was a professional soldier.

"Don't look so worried," Michelle whispered as they rounded a corner to reach their rooms.

Artus scratched his head. "*Shouldn't* we be worried?"

"Yes, of course," Michelle said as she opened the door. "But there's no reason to let *them* know that!"

Artus thought this over as he walked to a door flanked by two more of Myreon's eerie White Guard.

He took a deep breath. "Are you sure about this? You want it to be me?"

Michelle kissed his hand. "The Gray Lady insisted, and I agree with her. You are the only person here he will respect."

"He tried to kill me!"

"You're a prince, Artus—act like one." She stepped away from the door and waved him on. "You'll do fine!"

Artus straightened his cape and nodded to the guards. They stepped forward and threw open the doors. There, on the other side, in a bedroom watched over by two other White Guards, was Valen Hesswyn.

He was still muddy from the battle in the shallows

of the Fanning River the day before. He had a bandage over his head and his tunic was stained with blood. He had the expression of a man drained of all his vigor—like an invalid, resigned to death. He looked at Artus with dull eyes. "You. They would send you, wouldn't they?"

"I'm a prince. Nobody sends me anywhere," Artus lied. "How are you feeling?"

"Go to hell."

"Oh, so not that badly, then? Great—we were worried you'd caught quite a beating."

"We?"

"Myreon, Michelle, and I," Artus said. "You're lucky the White Guard were there to break it up—those peasant levies of yours were really planning to give you a stomping."

Valen sputtered. "What? White Guard?"

Artus jerked a thumb at the guards on either side of the door. "I'd say you should thank them, but I don't think they'd care much. C'mon—get up. Myreon wants to see you."

A flare of resistance lit behind Valen's eyes. Artus could see him weighing the risks of attacking him, of making a break for it. Artus tensed and moved his weight to the balls of his feet. He didn't want Valen to wind up killed by the White Guard, and if Valen made a move . . .

The moment passed. Valen seemed to come to his senses. "How's your stomach?"

The place where Valen had stabbed him—only barely healed—twinged slightly. Artus laughed despite himself. "Oh, is that you taunting me? Adorable. Come on, jackass—the Gray Lady hasn't got time for this."

He turned and walked away.

Valen had little choice but to follow. The White Guards fell into step on either side of him, matching his pace perfectly.

The palace was largely in ruins. Several grand galleries had collapsed, scorch marks peppered the walls, and rubble and bodies were still being cleared away by teams of commoners. In places, the sun shone through holes in the vaulted roofs. Though Artus had grown used to this over the past weeks, to Valen they were a revelation. The young knight stared, openmouthed, at the wreckage.

"I take it I'm to be ransomed, then?" Valen asked as they descended a half-crumbled marble staircase.

"Nope," Artus said absently as a beefy stonemason bowed to him and insisted on kissing his hand. Artus's skin crawled as it happened, but he let it happen anyway. He was supposed to be royalty, so here he was, being royal. When the man rose, he gave Valen an ugly look before returning to his repair work.

Valen gaped at them both. "What do you mean, 'nope'? Look at the damage done here! You *must* need money! My grandmother will pay!"

Artus winced. He had been hoping he wasn't going to be the person who had to say this. "Valen, your grandmother is dead. She didn't survive the battle at Fanning Ford."

Valen froze. "What? You . . . you didn't give her quarter?"

"She refused to surrender to our field commander, so he killed her."

The White Guards pulled open the grand doors to the Congress of Peers. Valen suddenly looked sick. He sank to one knee. "Why . . . why would she . . . why . . ."

Artus looked down at him, remembering at once that Valen was only a few years older than he was and that he had just learned that his grandmother—the most important person in his life—had been killed. No matter how much of a witch old Velia Hesswyn had been, that still had to hurt. He spoke softly, so that no one nearby could hear. "The field commander was a carpenter, Valen. Your mother refused to surrender to a carpenter. She tried to blast him with a wand, and so he had to kill her." Artus offered Valen a hand. "Which is where you come in."

Valen glared at the hand for a moment, but again some kind of internal battle was waged and, in the end, the civilized part of Valen won. He took the hand and allowed himself to be pulled to his feet. There was now something different about Valen—Artus could see it. His eyes were clearer now, his jaw set. *It's because he knows he's the Count now. That's all it took for him to be ready to accept that responsibility. Saints, what I wouldn't give to feel that certain of anything.*

The destruction inside the Congress was almost absolute. The benches were wrecked and burned, the floor was scorched and stained with blood, and part of the great domed ceiling had collapsed. At the far end of the great room, the Falcon Throne rested in pieces, scattered all across the dais. *Sahand's message to us all*, Artus thought.

A space had been cleared beneath the center of the dome. There stood Myreon, her blond hair ragged from lack of care. She wore gray robes that made her look like a beggar, but she was surrounded by people listening to her every word. At her side stood a short, broad man with a bald head and thick beard—Gammond Barth, the carpenter who had put an end to Velia Hesswyn. He had a war-hammer— the implement of the countess's demise—slung over his back. When he saw Artus and Valen come in, he nudged Myreon and pointed.

"Ah, Valen Hesswyn," she said, her voice clear. "So glad to see you're feeling better."

"Necromancer!" Valen shouted. "The Defenders will make you pay for this!"

Myreon didn't react to the threat. "I'm very busy and I don't have time to quarrel, so I will make this brief: House Davram is finished. Your army, such as it was, has either joined me or is lying dead on the banks of the Fanning River. Your knights and noble vassals are crushed and are currently resting in the dungeons of the Young Prince here. Your attempt to put down my revolution and restore the old order in Eretheria is over. In short, you have no bargaining position. Do you accept this?"

Valen stared at her, speechless.

Artus watched him for any sign of that reckless anger from earlier. "It's true, Valen. Don't say something stupid."

Valen looked at Artus. Artus did his best impression of a princely posture. Whatever he did, it had an effect on Valen. He swallowed hard and looked back at Myreon. "What . . . what is to become of me? My people? My family?"

"If I were to listen to the advice of some advisors," Myreon said, "I should execute you and all your bloodline as traitors to their own people. But I am not so bloodthirsty as all that." Over her shoulder, Barth scowled at Valen. *He* had been calling for Valen's head on a plate since his capture.

Myreon pressed on, "Instead, I want you to renounce the Hesswyns' claim to the County of Davram *in perpetuity*. You are no longer rulers there—Eretheria is changing, and there is no more room for petty tyrants fighting private wars every spring. Instead, you and your vassals will swear yourself to Prince Artus's service—you will become officers in his White Army, the army of Eretheria, of which I am general."

Valen looked as though he had just been stabbed. An expression of complete shock bled into one of absolute horror. Artus tried to put himself in Valen's shoes, but couldn't. Yes, he was being asked to give up his birthright and the birthrights of all his House, but so what? For all the years Artus had spent among the rich, he could never get used to how entitled they felt. Especially toward stuff they never earned.

Myreon watched Valen closely. Perhaps she saw some of his horror, perhaps she understood, but whatever the reason, her tone softened and she placed a hand gently on his shoulder. "Sahand is still abroad in Eretheria, Valen. He controls Ayventry—all of us are in danger. There is a future for you and your family, just not the same one as before. Join me—we could use your help, your advice. I am painfully short on people with real military training. We need you."

She reached into her robes and produced a piece of parchment—a declaration renouncing his claims that Artus knew she'd spent the better part of the night before drafting, stacks of Eretherian law books next to her desk. "We're winning this war, Valen. You can get on the winning side now, or rest with the losing side in the dungeons. What will it be?"

Valen looked down at the parchment. Everyone was staring at him—Artus knew if he signed that paper, it would be a terrible blow struck to every count and viscount and earl and petty lordling in Eretheria and beyond. It would be a nobleman not renouncing just his claims, but the claims of all his relations. The end of a way of life that stretched back centuries.

The truth was, they *needed* him to sign—Valen had more military experience than any of them, even at his age. He also could command the loyalty of a few dozen knights currently in the dungeons. Armored cavalry like that would be crucial in the war ahead.

But they were his enemies—had been his enemies as recently as yesterday. Artus couldn't see how this could go any way besides Valen ripping up that parchment and spitting on it.

To his complete surprise, Valen spoke to Artus next. "Do you vouch for this?"

"Wh . . . what?"

"Do you, Prince of Eretheria, vouch for everything she says? A future for me and my family? My personal safety and that of my vassals?"

"You have my word, Valen. And I've always been straight with you, haven't I?"

Valen reached a decision. He looked Myreon in the eye. "Get me a quill."

She smiled. "Get me a quill, *ma'am*."

CHAPTER 6

CRIMES OF WAR

The outskirts of Eretheria City had become one enormous armed camp. The levied soldiers of every peer, lord, and knight in Eretheria seemed to be pouring in from the countryside, their lords' pikes on their shoulders, and pitching tents or laying out blanket rolls on the nearest unoccupied patch of grass. Tabards of every color wandered the streets, all of them singing the praises of the Young Prince, the Gray Lady, or Good King Tyvian. Or all three at once.

Since the defeat of House Davram at Fanning Ford, Myreon's recruiting problems had been solved. Funding was also secure—Hool's vast wealth, left to Tyvian when she departed and then passed on to

Artus—was more than sufficient to arm and fund the revolution, at least in the short term. What remained was a far more difficult problem—logistics.

The first step involved organizing the volunteer soldiers into companies. As they were already familiar with the House system, that was where Myreon had started—men who arrived to volunteer in the army were directed to camp down with volunteers who once served the same House as they had. These five companies soon had to be divided into ten companies—there were *that* many of them. Myreon still had a couple of accountants counting heads, but she estimated she was leading an army of nearly three thousand men.

This first step led very quickly to a new problem—infighting. As it turned out, the Hadda boys weren't too fond of the Davrams, the Vora and the Camis groups fought like cats, and just about nobody liked the Ayventry bunch. That was to say nothing about the stragglers and wild hillmen and other ragtag bands that were scattered about, all of them lured to Artus's banner on the promise of an end to the campaign system and an overthrow of the five Houses that had pushed them out of society for so long.

Myreon's solution to this problem was similarly simple to the company organization: an enormous quantity of lye. All soldiers in her army were ordered to bleach their tabards white. Any house emblems were also to be thrown away. They were to be *one* army, she insisted. The White Army—the army that would save Eretheria. She didn't want men walking down the street and thinking they were "Hadda" men or "Vora" men—they were Eretherians.

The White Army had been laundering their clothing for two days now. The bleaching process was imperfect—even enchanted lye couldn't get *all* the color out of a green tabard, for instance. The visual effect was that the White Army was less actually white and more just plain drab. Observing her men from horseback as they floundered around a public fountain, the water frothing with soap, Myreon was starting to wonder at the wisdom of it all—just that morning her accountants had informed her of just how much she was spending on washing clothes and it was a breathtaking figure—but orders were orders, and if this whole army thing was going to work, she couldn't second-guess herself. She had to be strong, resolute. Artus might be the crowd-pleaser, but Myreon was the backbone. And the brains.

And pretty much everything else, to be honest.

"I've seen rebellions before, but never like this one." Myreon's breath caught at the voice—Argus Androlli. He was also on horseback, his staff in one hand. Somehow he'd managed to ride up next to her without any of her White Guard noticing. But of course, he was a mage. He could manage that.

Myreon resolved not to be flustered. "At least they'll be clean. In body, in spirit, in cause."

"Men are never clean. You were a Defender long enough to know *that*, Myreon."

Myreon smiled at him. "That's the past. I'm the future."

"We need to talk." Androlli looked at the volunteer soldiers surrounding them. A couple of men had picked up axes and spears and were giving the Mage Defender ugly looks. "Is there somewhere private we can go?"

Myreon held up a hand and the men with weapons paused. "You're not thinking of *arresting* me, are you, Argus?"

Androlli gave her a tight smile. "As you can see—I am alone. I'm not suicidal, Myreon. And I'm not about to burn a hundred peasants with wood-axes to ash to bring you in. I came to talk. I'm actually doing you a favor."

"Oh, yes—you're *famous* for your favors, Argus," Myreon said. "This way. We'll talk in my field tent."

Myreon motioned for some of the men to move aside, and move they did, though they didn't look happy about it. She and Argus rode side by side past rows of burned out houses and looted shops until they were out of the city entirely. Myreon's tent—a tall, gleaming white pavilion—was easy to spot among a sea of patched and yellowing canvas that comprised the ten companies of the White Army. As they rode there, volunteer soldiers hailed her as she passed, but no one challenged them. Other than a few chickens and careless children running around, they proceeded unhindered.

"You're mad, you know," Androlli said when they had at last dismounted. "This army—it's a joke, Myreon. You're going to get chewed apart."

"Argus, you know even less about armies than I do." Myreon snapped her fingers and the White Guards on either side of her tent's entrance pulled back the flaps. "Come in, before somebody out there tries to lynch you."

Androlli followed her inside, but not before giving the White Guard a long, disgusted look. The tent's interior was comfortable, if rustic, with a thick Rhondian carpet covering the muddy ground and a few portable folding chairs of hardwood and canvas. A large round table—also collapsible—occupied the center of the room. It was piled high with various correspondence and ledgers full of figures. Myreon waved her hand over them and laid a brief gibberish curse on it all—she didn't need Androlli reading her letters or reporting her supply figures back to Saldor.

This done, she sat down and summoned a White Guard to bring her a glass of water. "Well, what was it you wanted to discuss?"

Androlli nodded toward the white-clad, masked creature standing serenely behind her. "Do you really need to ask?"

Myreon was prepared for this, of course. That

didn't mean it was going to be pleasant. "I didn't create it, Argus. I'm merely controlling it."

"Hardly a nuance a Saldorian judge will appreciate," Androlli said, still standing.

"As I implied back at the fountain—you can't exactly arrest me, Argus. I'm in the middle of an armed camp—an armed camp full of men who think *the Defenders* killed their king and threw him off the top of a cathedral. You so much as poke one firepike out of Eretheria Tower, and the White Army will burn it to the ground."

"I already said I wasn't here to arrest you, Myreon. Necromancy is a crime, but it turns out it's not a severe enough crime to necessitate an international incident. Besides, it is the opinion of Lord Defender Trevard that it is better *you* lead the White Army than anyone else at the moment. Sahand is still a threat and still must be defeated. Until such time, it is the official decision of the Arcanostrum to remain neutral toward your little revolution."

"Then why are you here? Why are you wasting my time?"

"I came to warn you, Myreon," Androlli said. "There are limits to Saldor's patience."

"Meaning?"

"Meaning you cannot employ battlefield-scale sorcery and still expect Saldor to remain neutral. You can't deploy *those*," he pointed to the White Guard, "in a battlefield role and expect us not to intervene.

Battlefield necromancy has been forbidden for over a thousand years, Myreon. There's a *reason* for that."

Myreon chuckled. "The reason is that Saldor doesn't like anybody *else* using sorcery to win wars. That's it."

Androlli shook his head. "You sound like a radical, Myreon."

Myreon stood up. "I'm a mage leading an army of peasants in a revolution—you're damned *right* I'm a radical! And I won't have my victory dictated to by the likes of *you!*"

Androlli's face was red. "No more Fanning Fords, understand? No more undead legions engaging in battlefield roles! The Lord Defender nearly broke a rib, he yelled so much—he wanted you petrified for a full century over that. Some of the masters calmed him down a bit and many of the archmagi took your side, but the threat still stands. If you deploy sorcery like that again, Trevard will muster the Grand Army of Saldor and burn your foolish revolution to ash. Do I make myself clear?"

Myreon felt her heart thumping in her chest. "Yes, Argus. Perfectly clear."

Androlli took a deep breath. "Good."

"Get out."

Androlli snorted. "What, no escort out of the camp?"

Myreon tilted her head slightly and a pair of White Guards came to flank him. "There—happy now?"

Androlli's nostrils flared at the two animated corpses. "You can dress them up in white all you like, Myreon. You're still keeping company with the stolen corpses of the dead."

Myreon glared at him—a gesture that was sufficient to have the two White Guards practically frog-march Androlli out of her presence. She waited until she heard him mount up and ride off, the White Guards still escorting him. Then she let out a long, slow breath.

He was right. Fanning Ford had been a step too far, perhaps. It was one she had been forced to take—she never would have won the battle without them—but she had no excuse anymore. The living soldiers of her army now vastly outnumbered the dead ones, and it was for the best that way. Even with their white garb and masks, the constructs made the volunteers uneasy. The story about them being the bodies of former conscripted soldiers come back to help Eretheria win its freedom had helped a lot, but the sight of the White Guard in battle was too unnerving for the living to be fully comfortable. If she wasn't careful, they would sap morale, and if Fanning Ford had taught her anything, it was that morale was key. An army that was frightened was an inefficient army, and an army that ran away was no army at all.

She didn't have much time to think about it, though, before her role as general took over the rest of her day. She had Valen Hesswyn and his cavalry to attend to, she had company commanders to interview and appoint, she had supplies to requisition from . . . well, from somewhere, and a thousand other duties that kept her on her feet until the sun was well below the horizon.

Over dinner, the guild accountants delivered their report. "At this rate of expense, assuming the army grows no larger, you will run through the Royal Treasury in two months."

Myreon nearly choked on her wine. "That *can't* be true. How can that be true?"

The accountant was a young man in a starched ruff that extended past his shoulders, making it look as though his pointy head was being served on a white platter. His hands fiddled at his sides—he was evidently uncomfortable talking to a sorceress. "Please, Magus—the calculations are good. Food is . . . very scarce. And so it's become *unnaturally* expensive. In fact, *everything* is becoming more expensive for you . . . errr . . . *us*. Everyone knows you are—and pardon me for saying so—*desperate* for supplies, and quick. There's no competition."

Myreon tightened her fist. "I'm being cheated, you mean."

The accountant looked at his apprentices—two girls who seemed to have frozen in a permanent state of midcurtsey. They didn't meet his eye. He tugged at his collar. "The numbers are good, Magus. I'd swear by them."

"Then what do you recommend we do?"

The accountant stiffened. "I am not a military advisor, Magus. I couldn't possibly—"

"It wasn't a military question. It's a financial planning question." Myreon gave him a hard look. "Answer it."

"Well . . . if I were you, General Alafarr, I'd see about winning this war very quickly."

Myreon dismissed them with a growl. But the words stuck.

After dinner, she went down into the sewers. One last time.

The necromancer, whoever he had been, was long gone from his bloodstained haunts. Myreon assumed he had been killed in the battle for the palace. In any event, he had never reappeared. His grisly workshop and subterranean ritual space was hers now. Hers if it were anybody's.

The ritual had been running smoothly since it had been invoked. The great veta inscribed by the old blind necromancer still glowed with power, lighting the subterranean cavern as bright as midday—there was enough Lumenal energy to keep it running for months, perhaps years. Its power sustained the life force of all five hundred of the White Guard, and additions and small edits made by Myreon since then had expanded it so that, if need be, she could raise five hundred more. If she wanted, she could build even more on her already considerable power.

Yet Androlli was right; the White Guard were an abomination. They could and probably would serve to prevent her from achieving her goals. Necromancy, by its very nature, was wrong. This ritual had served its purpose. It was time for it to end.

It would be a relatively simple matter to disrupt the ritual. The bigger the ritual, the more delicate it was—a concentrated arc of Etheric energy and the whole thing would implode, just like Sahand's master Fey ritual in Daer Trondor had been undone by a snowball. Myreon was confident she could protect herself from the ensuing blast of Lumenal energy— she had dark thoughts aplenty to power an Etheric shield around herself.

Such dark thoughts, however, were what gave her pause. The accountants were *also* right—she needed to win this war. The challenges ahead of her were harrowing, indeed. Sahand's army had withdrawn from the city, yes, but it was still abroad in the countryside. Tales trickled into the camp daily—Delloran soldiers slaughtering villages, putting inns to the torch, stealing crops and livestock. Those people needed protection. It was why the White Army had come into existence in the first place.

To protect the people, Myreon needed to defeat Sahand. Sahand was a soldier with a lifetime of military experience. He had been conquering nations since before Myreon was born. His soldiers were well trained, blooded, and experienced. By all reasonable measures, Myreon and her White Army were doomed to failure.

Why, then, should she pass up any advantage? Why disrupt this ritual? So that she wouldn't anger Trevard? She was no Mage Defender anymore—who cared what that stiff old man thought?

If Sahand were in her place, would *he* dispel the ritual? Would *he* give up his one edge against his opponent?

Of course not.

Androlli had warned her not to use the White Guard in a battlefield role. Fine—there were probably numerous other uses for them. Uses she couldn't rely on others to fulfill.

Myreon subtly adjusted her stance before the ritual. She wasn't going to dispel it at all—no. Instead, she set about enchanting a linking stone, which would let her bring the power of the ritual with her, wherever she went.

When the White Army marched—and soon it certainly would have to—the ritual was coming along. And so, too, would come the White Guard.

CHAPTER 7

IN THE SHADOW OF SAHAND

The Citadel of Dellor was among the most ancient fortresses in the known world. Built to defend against foes unknown in ages long forgotten by some warlock king whose name was now lost to history, it was a vast, sprawling military structure—a five-pointed star of thick stone walls and flat defensive turrets squatting at the edge of the Great Whiteflood River.

There was no earthly reason to have a fortress this big in a land as remote as Dellor—it could have easily housed an army of well over ten thousand men, fully provisioned and not even forced to share cots in the seemingly endless barracks. However, there was also no feasible way to knock it down and many reasons it could be useful to a man like Banric Sahand.

Chief among these reasons was how impressive it was—the endless corridors filled with artfully concealed murder-holes and arrow slits, the cleverly disguised booby traps, and the many secret doors and passages belied a level of engineering ingenuity lost to the modern age. With every tour of the vast castle, Sahand was able to convey a very important message to just about anyone:

I am unassailable and thus invincible—remember this.

At that moment, the person being given this impression was a fleshy-cheeked young man—no, a *boy*—who, as it happened, was the sitting Count of Ayventry. He was a distant cousin to the late Count Andluss and the rest of Andluss's also-dead family. His trembling parents had presented him to Sahand two days before, and Sahand had taken an immediate liking to the puffy young dunce. He was stupid enough to have no idea he was being used and greedy enough to go along with whatever Sahand said, so long as it worked to his advantage. His name was Fawnse.

Sahand put an arm around the young count and guided him into the last stop on their tour—an underground, artificial harbor concealed within the fifth point of the Citadel's star. This point jutted into the river and, behind a huge stone gate, was an artificial waterfront big enough to accommodate ten huge barges, currently under construction.

Fawnse's eyes nearly popped out of his skull in surprise. "Wow! You have *ships*, too?"

Sahand smiled. "Those are just transport barges, Your Grace—without any good roads, the best way to explore the lands of Dellor is by river. The same goes for my troops. With these barges, I'll be able to keep my people safe from bandits and trolls and such."

Fawnse tipped his head upward, trying to encompass the whole of the vast vaulted ceiling in one glance and nearly falling over from the effort. "It's amazing!"

"So you see that I am a good friend to have, yes? Aren't you glad you came to visit?"

Fawnse nodded. "Oh, very much so! And to think my mother was so worried—she thought you were going to kill me!"

Sahand laughed. "I only kill my enemies, Fawnse— and you are no enemy of mine, are you?"

"No sir!" The boy answered, his eyes falling back to the barges and the swarm of workers hammering nails and sawing logs to aid in their construction. The vast chamber echoed with the sound of wood being bent to human use.

Sahand still had his arm around Fawnse. He gave the boy a hearty squeeze. "Fawnse, how are you liking being count?"

Fawnse smiled. "Fine, my lord. Just fine. My bed is huge!"

"So you wouldn't mind remaining count, then? For, say, a long time?"

"No, my lord!" Fawnse grinned. "It's been the greatest honor of my life!"

"And what are your thoughts on the so-called White Army—the upstart rebels who mean to usurp you?"

Fawnse snickered. "I have eight thousand levies and five hundred heavy cavalry that will *show* them what I think of them!"

Sahand nodded—the boy was overestimating his cavalry by at least a hundred fifty, but by no more than that. Add that to his own companies of light cavalry—two hundred strong—and the twelve companies of Delloran regulars and mercenaries he had in Eretheria, and that gave them an army of about four thousand men, give or take, plus those eight thousand worthless levies. Fawnse no doubt assumed he would be making his stand outside Ayventry, just as many other counts had over the years—wait until the enemy shows up, muster your armies on the broad fields surrounding the city, and have a very civilized pitched battle on some sunny summer afternoon.

This, of course, struck Sahand as a very stupid thing to do.

"Fawnse, I'm glad to hear you are a fighting man at heart. That is why I've made a strategic decision." He guided the boy out of the harbor and into a great hall where a vast round table had been set up and, upon it, an enormous map of Eretheria. Little wooden soldiers (for footmen) and horses (for cavalry) were scattered about the map—Sahand's troops were black, spread out like a net across the Eastern Basin and the Great South Plains, while Ayventry's were red, concentrated in the county at the very northern tip of the mountains and the basin. The forces of that resilient old hag, Ousienne of Hadda, were a smattering of yellow along Lake Country, which extended from the northern tip of the Tarralles to form the northern border of the Great South Plains. There, represented by a small cluster of white, still down by the coast near Eretheria City, was the White Army—the rebels who had made Eretheria an unsackable prize and forced Sahand's retreat north.

"My men are retreating north, as were my orders." Sahand gestured to his forces. "As they go, they are under orders to burn, loot, and pillage."

Fawnse frowned. "That isn't allowed, I thought."

"Ah, Fawnse—it is time I gave you an important lesson in statecraft: *everything* is allowed if no one can stop you." Sahand didn't wait to see if the boy understood or not. He pointed to the map, and specifically the two roads that ran north from Eretheria—the Freegate Road and the Congress Road. "When the Young Prince and his Gray Lady advance from Eretheria, they shall either travel up the Congress Road, which means they are headed for Lake Country, or the Freegate Road, which will take them directly to us. Either way they go, they will find no fodder on the land and only miserable, starving peasants in their way. This will force the Young Prince to slow down, to forage more widely, and to deal with the suffering of his own people."

Fawnse nodded slowly, squinting at the table. "What do my men do?"

Sahand pointed at the picture of a tower perched at the northern spur of the Tarralle Mountains, astride the Freegate Road. "Unless the White Army secures an alliance from Lake Country—which they will not—the only way to pass the Tarralles is under the ramparts of the castle of Tor Erdun."

Fawnse brightened. "The Earl of Tor Erdun is my uncle!"

Sahand nodded while the boy beamed at him. "So now you see what I want you to do with your men: take them—all of them—to Tor Erdun. Make certain your uncle is well supplied and stocked with fresh troops and take command of the garrison yourself. In a matter of weeks, a starving army of rebellious peasants and poor hedge knights will have to lay siege to it, and then my forces, which will have retreated into the mountains," Sahand moved a few black pieces into the Tarralles with a long stick, "will cut them off from behind. The rebellion will be crushed and you, Your Grace, will be the savior of Eretheria."

Fawnse clapped his hands and cheered. "A wonderful plan! I'll go and tell my captains right away!"

Sahand grinned. "Yes, do. My anygate remains open, linked to your castle. Come back and visit anytime, Fawnse!"

Fawnse bowed and left at a run. When he had gone, Sahand nodded to one of his lieutenants, who took care to bar the doors behind him and clear the hall of anyone but Sahand's inner circle. "Inform my companies to fall back toward Ayventry. I want the city fully garrisoned by my own armies once Count Fawnse's troops have gone."

His men leapt into action, pulling out sending stones and seeking to make contact with Sahand's farflung forces. As they worked, Sahand folded his arms behind his back and strolled onto the balcony that overlooked his secret harbor. There, the large, square barges were halfway complete. They would be able to ferry over a thousand men across the Whiteflood in a single trip—an invasion force.

One of his captains was beside him at the rail. "Sire, won't the boy tell people about these barges? Won't he reveal your plans?"

Sahand arched an eyebrow at the man—he was young, newly promoted. Perhaps a little overbold in speaking with his prince. Still, Sahand was in a jovial mood. "I do not show my plans to fools, Captain."

The captain puzzled this over for a moment, chewing his moustache. "A clever ruse, sire."

Sahand seriously doubted the fellow had any idea what he was talking about. He laughed. "That includes you, too, Captain." Sahand slapped him on the back. "Now, bring me Arkald the Strange. We need to discuss my prisoner."

Arkald the Strange, personal necromancer to Prince Banric Sahand, could not sleep. No matter how many fur blankets he piled upon his bed, no matter how well he stoked the iron stove in his small chamber, no matter what potions he concocted to ease his way into slumber, he lay shivering and awake each and every night, his eyes wide open. Staring upward. Knowing that, on the floor just above him, a nightmare walked. And waited. And plotted.

No amount of pleading was able to dissuade the Mad Prince from using the top floor of Arkald's tower for a prison. Never mind that it was Arkald's preferred ritual space. Never mind that it was incoherently dangerous to keep the prisoner alive. He had thrown himself on his face before Sahand, tugging at the hem of his fur cape. "Please, Your Highness! Kill her! Just kill her, I beg of you! For all of our sakes!"

Sahand had only grinned at him. Always fearsome, Sahand's smiles held something extra special these days—one cheek had been torn away in battle, and now one could see his teeth all the way back to his molars on one side. When he smiled, he seemed part crocodile. "No, Arkald. One does not destroy so useful a vessel of knowledge as this. Certainly not out of fear. She is to be your captive and you her jailor."

"No!" Arkald had gasped.

Still that horrible, half-human smile. "Yes, Arkald. I trust your terror of her is sufficient to make you a very *efficient* and *thorough* guardian of our permanent guest. And of course, I don't need to tell you what happens if she dies in your care, do I?"

What could Arkald say? He touched his forehead to the stone floor of Sahand's throne room and swore it would be done.

The ritual space at the top of Arkald's tower had been Astrally warded. Arkald had spent days etching the runes on the outside of the tower, using a rickety wooden scaffold that hung from the tower's roof and suspended him hundreds of feet in the air. When they were complete, the runes rebuffed all the energies except the Astral—the fifth energy, the medium through which the other four moved. Any sorcery based in the four—Ether, Lumen, Fey, or Dweomer—would be impossible.

As for the Astral, Sahand had assured Arkald that the prisoner was sufficiently mutilated to make any significant spellcraft impossible. Arkald, of course, did not believe this for a moment, and so every day he made a point of siphoning as much of the Astral as he could into a ritual of his own—a spell to unwrite and then rewrite books by locally reversing and then advancing the flow of time. Such a spell was enormously taxing—so much so that Arkald's own work and study had to fall by the wayside—but it was essential. His survival depended on it. If that woman were able to cast even a single spell . . .

And so, Arkald the Strange did not sleep. His appetite left him. He feared what wine or beer might do to his wits, and so he refused these, as well. Within a week, he appeared every bit as skeletal as any of his creations ever had.

Once a day, Arkald mustered all of his modest courage and made the ascent up the claustrophobic spiral staircase to what he had come to call "the cell," carrying a light wooden tray with bread, cheese, and a pitcher of water. He took care to carry no weapon and left all his charms and rods and wards behind. They would do him no good in any case.

The cell itself was fourteen feet across. There was nothing in the room save a stool, a clay chamber pot, and a pile of dirty straw. The trap door to the roof had been nailed shut, and the only window had been fixed with inch-thick iron bars. Through this poured the morning sunshine, bathing the sparse chamber in a cheery orange glow.

There, huddled within a threadbare robe and sitting upon the stool in the full light of day, was Lyrelle Reldamar—the most terrifying woman in the world.

She had been roughly used in her journey to Dellor. Her thumbs were missing and one eye was still swollen shut. Her face was an array of yellowing bruises, and her hair—once the color of spun gold—was torn and matted and dirty. Each night up here, with no fire to warm her, must have been hellishly cold; Arkald could see it in how her shoulders shivered at the slightest breeze.

And yet, each morning she smiled at him. "Good morning, Arkald. How are you today?"

Arkald placed the wooden tray on the floor, staying well out of arm's reach. He circled her, his back to the wall.

Lyrelle watched him, her keen eyes tracking him like a cat tracks a mouse. "I must apologize again for imposing upon you. I know how important your work must be to you."

Arkald frowned and picked up the chamber pot, carrying it to the window. He said nothing, even though he wanted to yell at her. No, more than that—he wanted to rush downstairs, get a knife, and stab this woman through the heart. Then she would be dead and gone and out of his life forever. Gods, the League might even forgive him for the death of Renia Elons and then he could escape this tower and Sahand and go far, far away. Somewhere quiet. Somewhere no one would bother him again.

"Your silence betrays you, Arkald," Lyrelle said as he dumped the contents of the pot out the window. Thanks to the bars it was, as ever, a messy job. A splash of cold urine dripped over the sill and trickled to the floor.

Arkald stepped back and inspected his robe and shoes, making sure nothing had spattered on him. "Be quiet!" he snapped, but his voice didn't come out quite as the bark he'd wanted it to. It was more of a bleat, a pathetic honking sound.

"Why, Arkald, if I cannot speak with you, with whom can I?"

Arkald wrung his hands. "No one. You can remain silent. Say nothing!"

Lyrelle frowned. "That seems needlessly unpleasant for both of us." When Arkald stiffened, she went on, "Clearly this is an ordeal for you as well as me. Surely a bit of civilized conversation would not be out of order."

Arkald began to circle back toward the door. "Hurry up and eat or I will leave and you will go hungry."

Lyrelle drew her head up. Her glamours were gone and she had not sipped *cherille* in some time, but even still—even with the wrinkles beginning to grow at the corners of her eyes and the white beginning to streak through her hair—there was something regal about her. She made Arkald feel as a donkey in the presence of a parade horse. "If you take my food, I would starve."

"What is that to me?"

"I am an old woman, Arkald—two decades your senior, I should think—and my health in this frigid prison is not the best. Were I to take ill as a result of malnourishment, I could die."

Arkald frowned. "I have healing poultices. Illbane powder."

"None of which will function in this room." Lyrelle raised an eyebrow. "Do you mean to suggest you would remove me from this tower, even for an instant? Even to save my life?"

Arkald said nothing, but his scowl probably said enough.

"I thought not. So, as you are unwilling to starve me and as *I* am unwilling to eat without some manner of conversation, I suggest you remain and chat a while as I enjoy this feast you have brought me."

"It's a trick. You're trying to trick me."

Lyrelle smiled. "Oh, Arkald—of *course* it's a trick. But I've played it, see? I have forced you to talk with me while I eat. Not so very sinister, is it?"

Arkald looked at the tray, the pitcher. "I could just leave and come back later!"

"And leave me with a clay pitcher with which to brain you as you come through the door? Now, now, Arkald—that seems risky, don't you think?"

Dammit, the woman had a point. He shuffled his weight from foot to foot. "What would we talk about?"

"Assuming the doings of your master are not up for discussion, nor are suggestions for how to escape this efficient little trap you've set, I'm afraid I don't have much to discuss. The rumor mill up here is rather . . . sparse." She scooped up the bread with one four-fingered hand. "Why don't you tell me about yourself?"

"No."

Lyrelle took an awkward bite. "No? Very well, why don't you tell me what it's like to work for Banric Sahand."

Arkald shook his head. "That's a bad idea."

Lyrelle chuckled. "Oh, Arkald—worried I might tattle on you to your prince? Please. That old brute would never believe a word I said. Come now. Unburden yourself. You and I could spend the day telling each other all the various things we hate about Banric Sahand, and nobody—least of all Sahand himself—would ever be the wiser. When else will you have an opportunity like that?"

Arkald opened his mouth and then . . . stopped. This was it—this was how it started. This was how she was going to get inside his head. "You are going to stay here until you die. If you want to spend the day without water, that's up to you. I won't be made into your tool."

He marched over, quite close to her, and picked up the pitcher and the tray, throwing the cheese onto the ground.

Lyrelle fell to her knees, clutching at his robes with her mutilated hands. The regal woman from moments before was gone—a wild, miserable desperation filled her face. "Oh, please, no! No, Arkald! Leave me the water, please! I'm sorry!"

Arkald pulled himself free as though he were being bitten and fled the room, slamming and barring the door behind him. From inside, he heard his prisoner begin to sob.

He knew that kind of cry. He had cried that way himself many times since being brought here. They were tears of despair. They hurt him to hear, but he tarried by the door anyway to listen. Perhaps it was an act—a trick.

Lyrelle Reldamar wept for almost an hour. She screamed. She cursed Sahand and her son, Xahlven. She beat weakly on the door. Then, eventually, Arkald heard her lie in the straw and slowly cry herself to sleep.

Then, on wobbly legs, Arkald descended to his own room—his own cell—and sat before the book he had forced time to unwrite and rewrite endlessly. His hands trembling, he began the ritual again.

"Necromancer!" A voice bellowed from the stairs below—a guard. "The prince wishes to see you!"

A bolt of fear struck through Arkald's throat. It took him a moment to find his voice again. "Yes. I'm . . . I'm coming."

The guard waited for him. Like most of Sahand's men, he was a meaty block of a human being in a mail shirt. Standing next to him, Arkald felt like a little boy about to be spanked by his father. The guard said almost nothing—only grunted and poked him in the back with the butt of his spear when he wanted Arkald to walk faster.

The Citadel of Dellor was too huge to heat effectively, and so it was a long, cold journey down the stairs of Arkald's tower and through the long galleries and cavernous halls to Sahand's private chambers. The doors were tall and studded with iron, their latches fashioned in the shape of a wyvern's claws. There were two guards posted on either side of them, as usual, as mail-clad and humorless as the guard who'd fetched him. Arkald's escort prodded the necromancer forward. "The necromancer, as ordered."

The two soldiers opened the doors and motioned for Arkald to go in. Holding his breath, Arkald forced himself to pass over the threshold into Sahand's inner sanctum. The doors boomed closed behind him.

He was alone.

Or, more accurately, he was alone with Banric Sahand.

Sahand's private parlor was decorated with the faded banners of the many mercenary companies and petty lords he had crushed on the fields of battle over the years. They hung from the high rafters and along the walls, all of them varying degrees of tattered and bloodstained, many charred, and some so faded that their devices were barely recognizable. At the other end of the room was a high-backed chair of dark wood, carved into the image of a wyvern rising in flight—an echo of the great chair of steel that stood in the Mad Prince's formal throne room. This one looked rather more comfortable, which had the perverse effect of making it somehow more sinister—Sahand preferred to *relax* in a chair that looked like a monster and surrounded by the tattered remnants of his enemies.

A hunk of bloody meat and a goblet of what was probably oggra rested on a table before Sahand's chair. Sahand was using a wicked-looking dagger to slice off chunks of the red meat and spear them to be popped into his mouth. There was no chair for Arkald. Indeed, there was no other furniture at all apart from a huge manticore-skin rug that stretched from the doors to the foot of Sahand's table.

Arkald stood perfectly still, as though trying not to wake the manticore rug.

It was a full minute before Sahand looked at him. When he did, he pointed the knife at him and waved it to indicate the necromancer should come closer. Arkald went halfway across the rug and stopped. "You called for me, sire?"

Sahand chewed his meat with gusto, his ruined cheek giving Arkald a perfect view of the process. Red juice squirted across the table. "You don't bow, Arkald. Why is that?"

Arkald instantly fell to his knees and abased himself. "I'm sorry, sire. I . . . I forgot . . . please . . ."

Sahand laughed, the bloody remnants of his meal leaking from the holes in his face and staining his close-cropped beard. "Stand up, stand up—if I cared so much about protocol from you, I'd have killed you long ago. It's enough to see you shiver when you're in my presence."

His heart pounding, Arkald staggered back to his feet. "As you say, sire."

Sahand dabbed at his face with a bloodstained handkerchief and took a careful sip of oggra. "Tell me about Lyrelle."

Arkald's breath caught. He couldn't *know* what she said to him, could he? This . . . this was just chance, yes? He licked his lips. "She . . . she suffers greatly, sire."

Sahand sawed off another chunk of meat. "Good— I'm glad of it. And her health?"

"She . . . she appears sickly, sire. She may catch ill, given the cold."

Sahand paused. "Is that a note of concern I hear, Arkald?"

"No! No sire!"

Sahand frowned at him. "So you're saying you don't care if she dies?"

A bolt of terror shot through him again. A trap—it was a trap! "I . . . I mean, yes, of course I *care* but . . . but . . . but only because *you* commanded me to keep her alive and . . . and . . . so therefore I care, but not *really.*"

Sahand laughed at him. "You are to provide her no comforts, understood? Not so much as a new blanket. If I learn you have been coddling her, I'll take *your* thumbs as well."

Arkald remembered to bow this time. "Yes, sire."

Sahand returned to eating for a moment, leaving Arkald standing there. Arkald's stomach rumbled. It occurred to him that he hadn't eaten all day. Even before Lyrelle Reldamar had played havoc with his appetite, food was difficult to come by for Arkald—Sahand did not pay him. He was not in Sahand's employ in any economic sense—he was Sahand's permanent guest. He had to barter for food from the kitchens, and few people there had much interest in feeding a necromancer. He'd lived on crusts of bread, pork gristle, and thin soup for years now. Sometimes he managed a little beer or wine, but only if he stole it.

It occurred to Arkald that Sahand was eating in front of him on purpose. Every hunk of meat the Mad Prince swallowed was just another reminder of Arkald's absolute inferiority—of his servile wretchedness. He could do nothing but watch, his empty stomach groaning.

"What does she say?" Sahand asked at last.

"Sire?"

Sahand was looking at Arkald intently. "About me, about anything—what does she say?"

Arkald shivered—a draft from somewhere, or so he told himself. Here was the moment he could tell Sahand about Lyrelle's attempt to turn him. Perhaps . . . perhaps Arkald's show of loyalty would be rewarded somehow. Sahand *did* reward him from time to time. Perhaps he could ask for some payment or new clothing or even an assistant or something.

"Well, Arkald?"

Arkald realized that he had not said anything yet. He opened his mouth. "She . . ." he trailed off.

"Yes?"

"She weeps, sire. She curses your name and her sons." Arkald took a deep breath. "She despairs."

Sahand glared at him for a moment. Arkald tensed, awaiting the violent backlash for the lie. What bones would the Mad Prince break this time?

But Sahand only smiled. "Good. Very good." The Mad Prince waved him away. "You may go, Arkald. Give me regular reports."

Arkald bowed and took his leave, uncertain of what he said in response—probably "yes sire." He was out in the halls and alone a minute later. He ducked into a sawtooth alcove—some ancient defensive measure—and tried to slow his heart from racing. He'd lied. He'd lied to Banric Sahand.

And he'd gotten away with it!

Arkald wept.

But this time with relief.

CHAPTER 8

DARK TIMES

Myreon stood amid the ruins of the little village, flanked by her White Guard. At her feet was the body of a little boy, his head smashed. She could scarcely look at him. There was nowhere better to look.

Barth's scouts had spotted the smoke at dawn as the White Army moved north. True to her plan, she had insisted the army keep moving—the scouting party would catch up later. Myreon had also insisted on inspecting the ruins in person. "If I'm fighting a war," she had said to the old carpenter, "I should at least know what it costs." As she looked at the body of the little boy, facedown in the mud, she now had her answer.

But there was no going back now. There was no going back the moment she signed the necromancer's contract in the sewers. This path—this war—was going to be her legacy, her life's work. The cost in blood had to be worth it. She would *make it* worth it.

Barth, wearing a dented breastplate intended for a smaller man and a feathered cap intended for a larger one, came out of one of the more intact houses and went to Myreon's side. His face was still, but his eyes were full of barely constrained rage. "There were some survivors. Found 'em in a root cellar—women and children." He shook his head and took a few deep breaths. He wiped at his eyes.

"Who did it?" Myreon was surprised at how calm her voice was. Her years of sorcerous training, she supposed—one's emotions needed to be under control, or else the Fey leaked into all of one's incantations.

Barth spat. "The Ghouls. On Sahand's personal orders, I shouldn't wonder."

"How many dead?"

"About a hundred or so. Half of them unarmed." Barth's voice cracked. "Just farmers! Gods, Magus! How much more of this have we got to stand, eh? This is the fifth village hit, and that's just what we've heard of! Hann's mercy . . ." He shook his head and snuffled. "These aren't men we're fighting. Not men."

Myreon laid a hand on his shoulder. She tried to think of something inspiring to say, but there was nothing. She just left her hand there, and the old carpenter let it stay as his hulking shoulders shook with silent tears for a moment. Finally, he wiped beneath his eyes and took a long breath. "When . . . when this all started, Magus. When I fought with you in Eretheria, you promised a better world. This isn't better."

Myreon took her hand away. "I know, Barth. I'm sorry."

A peasant soldier, tall and lanky, ran up. After a wary eye at the silent White Guard, he pressed a knuckle to his temple in salute. "General, we've collected the dead . . . except . . ." His eyes strayed to the dead child.

Myreon stepped back. "Yes, of course. When they are together, leave them. The White Guard will bury the bodies."

The peasant soldier gently lifted the dead little boy and walked away. The man's face was pale, his eyes sunken.

Barth grunted. "It ain't natural, having the dead bury the dead. There should be a priest. There should be friends and family. Wine to ease the passage."

Sahand is counting on us slowing down, on us burying our dead. He uses our decency as a weapon against us. Myreon didn't say this, though. She changed the subject. "Which way did the Ghouls go?"

Barth shrugged. "Seems like they cut across country, though I can't say why. Those bastards set a hell of a pace—we can't match it, especially not off the roads."

"So they get away," Myreon said.

"So they get away. Again." Barth said, his voice tight.

It had been the way ever since they set march—Sahand's army, working in small bands and in supernatural coordination, scattered across the countryside, burning and pillaging but never engaging in battle. It was a bizarre, perverse strategy. No one on her command staff had ever seen the like of it before. But of course, none of them were really soldiers. Even Valen Hesswyn barely qualified.

Sahand, on the other hand . . .

"You're dismissed, Barth," Myreon said. "Catch up to the army. I'll be back by sundown."

Barth nodded and left, pulling himself awkwardly into the saddle of a sturdy pony and trotting away. The men in the scouting party went with him, their heads bowed, their bleached tabards stained with blood and ash.

Soon there was only Myreon and the White Guard. She had brought fifteen of them, and with a tap of her staff, those fifteen silently moved to just beyond the village, where the dead had been laid out in the afternoon sun. Myreon passed the women and the children, doing her best to separate the horror of their deaths from the fact of their bodies. That was how she had to think of them now—merely inert objects, decaying matter. She willed the White Guard to begin digging the grave—one great trench into which all these people would be rolled and then covered.

Then Myreon came to the men. These she examined more closely, walking down the line and trying to judge age and height and the extent of their injuries. She found twenty of them who were more or less intact and who were of approximately the right frame and size. She had the White Guard separate out these and arrange them in a wide circle, foot to toe.

The first of the two spells she intended to cast was a desiccation spell that would eliminate the fluids in the corpses, effectively mummifying them. This was difficult work, as the sun was strong and the Ether weak in the area, but she had done this several times now and was getting rather good at it. The process took two hours.

Then came the easy part. Myreon removed the linking stone from her belt purse—a small crystal orb that glittered with the sunny power of the Lumen. With a few words and a little coaxing of the ample Lumenal energy in the grassy field, the dead men of the destroyed village rose as one. They were met by a White Guard who held out a box of tunics and volto masks. At her urging, the newly risen dead dressed in their new garb—white shrouded, masked, and ready to serve.

"I'm sorry," she said to the dead, despite herself. "I'm so sorry to do this to you. You deserved better."

The animated corpses, of course, had nothing to say. They fell into a column behind her, marching with eerie precision. Her steps heavy, she turned away from the village and began the long journey to meet with the White Army. Behind her, the only things that moved in the ruined village were the bodies of dead men burying dead women and children.

Though she was surrounded, she was also alone. She realized she was often alone now. People's eyes did not shine for the Gray Lady as they once had. No one embraced her, or asked for her blessing, or beseeched Hann on her behalf. Necromancers did not receive such welcomes, even if their efforts were for the good. Even Artus . . . well . . . they had never been close, she and Artus. And Tyvian's death and what had happened in the palace had only alienated him further from her. Now he had Michelle and the adoration of the peasantry to occupy most of his time anyway.

No, Myreon was alone. Alone to bear the terrible burdens this "war" was laying on her shoulders. She had no one to confide in, no one to weep with. She had to be seen as stronger than everyone. Her arts and Artus's gleaming reputation were what made the White Army function, and no crack could be shown in that facade. And so she wept in moments like this—when she was alone but for the abominations she herself had helped create, and where no one would ever see.

Barth was right—this *was* worse. The initial euphoria of their early victories was long gone, wiped away by the march north. The spring campaigns might have ended, but this war was a darker thing than they had ever been. No Eretherian lord ever burned the fields of his enemies. No Eretherian knight sacked villages or permitted his men to rape women or murder children. It was undreamed of. Even when Perwynnon rode against Sahand the first time, their battles had observed the conventions of the Common Law. But now, all bets were off along the Great South Plains. Sahand had no compunction about running a war that made people suffer on purpose, and it was just this lack of decency that was going to let him win.

Their only chance was to get to Tor Erdun, and soon—to take the pass before Sahand could fortify it. So she drove her army onward, refusing to let Valen pursue this or that mercenary company as they tried to coax the White Army into a pointless chase in the Eretherian hinterland. But every village they found like this slowed them down, and every order she gave forbidding action sapped morale. They were low on supplies already, and morale was perhaps even lower.

Her army needed a victory—needed it so badly she felt as though the fate of all of Eretheria, or decency *itself* hung in the balance. And she would do anything—*anything*—to secure that victory.

She marched into the gathering dusk with her undead soldiers all around her.

She would make it worth it. She would make it all worth it.

Artus put his hand at the level of his cheekbone. "He would be about this tall, with red hair. If you heard him speak, he'd sound like a lord, but with a foul tongue. He'd probably be wearing a sword—a rapier."

The three peasants kneeling on the floor of Artus's tent exchanged glances. They were a father and his two sons who'd been on a harrowing journey—first fleeing from the Peregrine Palace, then dodging Sahand's men in the fields, and finally finding their way to the White Army. They were haggard with travel, but had insisted on being brought to see the Young Prince. Artus had barely waited for them to kiss his ring before he started asking questions.

The father cleared his throat. "If I had news of that kind, Your Highness, I would tell you for sure. But . . . no, sire. We've seen no such man."

Artus nodded. He'd known the answer as soon as he saw their faces. He knew that they knew what he was asking, too. He bade them rise. "I'm sorry for everything you've been through, really I am." He reached for his purse.

The father bowed. "Begging your pardon, sire, but we'll not take a copper from you."

Artus blinked. "But you must need it. Please."

All three shook their heads. The father had tears in his eyes. "You don't understand, my prince. It's not you who owes us. No sire. It's . . ." He sniffled. "It's us who owes you."

Artus took the man's hand and shook it. He put a hand on his shoulder. "If you need anything, let me know. And thank you."

All three of them teared up then. They all knelt again before leaving, muttering blessings and invoking Hann's name on his behalf. When they at last retreated through the flap of the tent, Artus fell back into his chair. He rubbed his face—he felt like he'd just run a mile. "Gods and saints . . ."

Michelle came from behind a curtain in the tent that walled off her bedchamber. She pressed a goblet into Artus's hand. "You know money isn't going to solve their problems, Artus."

"What else can I do? What else can I offer them?" He gestured to his fine clothes and the sumptuous tent that surrounded them. "How can I be living like *this* and they think it's an insult to take my coin?"

"You're *prince*, Artus—you *deserve* all this." Michelle sat in a chair next to him. "You need to start acting as your station commands."

Artus scowled. "The hell I do! I'm not a lordling! I'm not like Valen . . ."

Michelle pursed her lips—a sign that she was angry. "Valen isn't like you, no. Valen *wishes* he were like you. You're a natural leader, Artus. You have the bearing of royalty. You need to stop acting like a peasant."

Artus knew he should have left it at that—he knew he could walk away and just let the statement hang, but he couldn't. He thought of his mother, his sisters—all so far away, across the mountains, living in a four-room farmhouse. "I *am* a peasant, Michelle. It's in my blood! I'm no more a king than those three are!"

Michelle paled. "Don't *say* that, Artus! I know you grew up in common surroundings, but you *mustn't* lower yourself like that!"

Artus took a sip of wine. "And why not? What's so bad about being common?"

"Because people don't die for *common* men!" Michelle snapped. "Because you are leading an *army* that believes in you! Do you know how much of this army's cohesion relies on their opinion of you? Do you think *Myreon* commands their loyalty? No—it's you, Artus. Only you."

Artus froze, staring at her. Gods, she was *right*, wasn't she? Everybody was counting on him to be . . . to be what? He was a farmboy and a cutpurse and a pretty decent tail and a more than decent brawler, but a prince? It was absurd. *Tyvian, what the hell did you get me into?*

Michelle took his hand and squeezed it. "You are doing fine, Artus. You're doing just fine."

"I don't belong here, Michelle. I'm not cut out for this."

She grinned and kissed him on the nose. "Then it's a good thing I'm here to tell you what to do."

The tent flaps opened and Valen ducked inside. He looked out of breath. "Artus . . . Your Highness, I mean."

Artus stood up. Valen's face was grim. "What? What is it?"

Valen motioned for Artus to follow. "You'd better come see this."

Valen filled Artus in on the vague story of how Barth's scouting parties had caught the Delloran—the accounts Valen had received varied widely—but what was certain was this: he had been a member of the Ghouls and he had almost certainly been left behind. He had a nasty arrow wound in his thigh that had become infected despite being bandaged. Evidently, the Ghouls felt the cost of amputating a leg and feeding the crippled man indefinitely was too high, and they'd dumped him.

Much of this, though, Artus had to piece together later. He *should* have heard it firsthand, but instead of bringing the man to him for questioning, the soldiers of the White Army had kept him for themselves.

The Delloran, stripped naked, was in the middle of a ring of jeering White Army volunteers. He was delirious with infection, his nose was broken and eyes nearly swollen shut from the beating he'd received. On three sides of him, their teeth bared and growling, were three hunting dogs. Somehow, they were the least feral element of the scene.

The Delloran swatted at the dogs as they darted in and out, testing him. He couldn't stand and was therefore rolling around on his back, his whole body trembling. The peasants roared for blood. One of the dogs rushed in and caught a hold of the Delloran's hand in its jaws and began to worry it back and forth. The Delloran screamed, blood pouring down his arm, his other hand beating ineffectually on the dog's head. Another dog got a piece of his good leg—by the thigh—and began to drag the Delloran along in the mud with short, sharp tugs. The man's screams were mingled with barely coherent pleas, then names Artus couldn't recognize, and appeals to Hann's mercy.

Artus had seen enough. "Hey! Stop! Stop it!"

No one heard him. Nobody paid the least attention. They were chanting for blood, their eyes fixed on the grisly scene, shouting themselves raw. Artus wished he had a horse, but it was too late to have one fetched—the prisoner would be dead before then.

Fine—the old-fashioned way it is. Artus pushed aside a man at the back. When he tried to slap Artus back, Artus caught his arm, twisted it, punched him just beneath the nose hard enough to knock out teeth. The man dropped like an empty sack. The next two men Artus pushed apart with each hand on a shoulder. They went to curse him, but then noticed who he was and recoiled. A third man—this one close to the action—jabbed his elbow back at Artus's face. Artus ducked it, kicked him in the back of the knees and grabbed him by the hair.

By this point, word had spread—the Young Prince was here and he wasn't happy. A hush fell over the crowd. They fell to one knee almost as one. The only sound left was the snarling of the dogs—the Delloran had passed out.

Artus dragged the peasant he had by the hair into the ring and threw him facedown in the dirt. Then he drew his sword and, with three quick strokes, killed the dogs. "Whose dogs were these?"

Silence.

"I asked you all a *question!*" Artus searched the bowed heads for some sign of the guilty party, but there was nothing. He couldn't even see their faces.

Artus kicked the man at his feet. "You—explain yourself!"

"Begging your pardon, Your Highness, but . . . but . . ."

Artus whacked his arse with the flat of his sword. "Out with it!"

"He's a Delloran, sir!" The man squealed, "He's only a Delloran!"

"He's a man!" Artus yelled. "And you were going to feed him to the dogs? A human being?"

Again that still, sullen silence. Artus didn't need them to speak—he knew what they were thinking. *But they've done the same to us. To our children. To our wives.*

He looked down at the naked Delloran. He still lived, but only barely. He nodded toward the White Guard, who had been waiting patiently at the crowd's edge for orders. "Take him to the healers. I want him to be able to talk to us, and soon."

The white-robed undead stepped forward quietly and picked up the Delloran between the two of them with no sign of strain. The crowd of peasant militia parted for them as though their state was contagious. Artus glared at them. "I want you all to think about this: What makes you better than the Dellorans, anyway?" Artus held up his bloodied sword. "As of this moment, it's one thing less than before. Take care you don't become the thing you hate." He wiped the blade of his sword on a peasant's back, leaving a streak of blood, and sheathed it. "Where is Gammond Barth? Have him sent to my command tent straightaway!"

Valen gave Artus a cruel grin. "With pleasure, sire."

Artus stepped over the bodies of the dogs and left, not looking back. Behind him, the silence remained.

Later, in the command tent, Valen brought in Barth as though he were a bouncer escorting a man out of a bar. When Artus related what had happened, Barth shrugged. "You might think I can tell these men what to do, Your Highness, but I don't. Not all the way. The men said they was going to take him to you. I believed them."

Artus wasn't buying it. "The hell you did, Barth!

You know better than anybody how angry the men are—you *knew* this would happen!"

Valen nodded, his arms crossed. "I want names, Barth. Those men are to be hanged."

Barth sneered at Valen. "And what, then the White Army starts decorating the trees with Eretherian bodies? Just how much rope do you think we have, rich boy?"

Valen took a step toward Barth, his hand falling to his sword. "These men violated the conventions of war!"

Barth stepped right up to the young knight, nose to nose. "Kroth's teeth, you naive ponce! There *are* no bloody conventions of war—Sahand keeps proving that, day in and day out! The more you cling to your toy soldier ideals, the worse this is going to get."

"Toy soldier ideals? My men are the only real soldiers in this entire army! Unless they learn some discipline, *your* peasant mob is going to be the death of us all!"

Artus stepped between them and pried them apart. "Stop it, both of you! We're only a few days out from Tor Erdun—we can't afford to lose either of you in some stupid brawl!"

Valen retreated to a chair and sat down, pouring himself a cup of water from a clay pitcher. He put his elbows on his knees and leaned forward. In the flickering lamplight, he looked haggard—much older than his eighteen years would imply. "We need to do *something*."

Barth also found a chair, but on the opposite side of the tent. He was squinting at the map in the dim light. "The closer we get to Tor Erdun, the more we're bumping into Sahand's forces. I keep getting reports—unconfirmed, mind, but I believe them. We're close. If we send out a probing force, we might just be able to engage someone or something."

"That isn't the general's plan," Artus pointed out.

Barth spat. "Hang the Gray Lady, and pardon me for saying so. She's bloodless as a witch. Her plan's all well and good for beating Sahand, I suppose, but it won't do nothing for all those poor souls what he's burned out of house and home!"

Valen nodded slowly. "You know I hate to admit this carpenter is right about anything, Artus—*sire*—but he's right about this. You are prince. This is *your* army, not hers."

Artus looked between the two of them—Valen was right, they hardly ever agreed. Here it was, then—the thing Michelle had been saying. *His* army. He was prince. At his word, they would all do whatever he said. Right now, they wanted permission to go tearing off after some splinter of Sahand's army—on a bloody gnome hunt—and where would that get them? Maybe some satisfaction, but beyond that? Nothing. It was what Myreon said Sahand wanted them to do.

Barth had his hands balled into fists. "Only give the word, sire! We'll bring the bastards to justice!"

"I don't think so . . ."

Valen grabbed Artus by the upper arm and shook him, as though trying to wake him up. "Take *command*, sire! Stop doing whatever that sorceress tells you to!"

What would Tyvian do? Artus wondered. It was a question he asked himself daily, but he never seemed to come up with a reasonable answer. Long-term plans were always Tyvian's forte. *Pretending* he was Tyvian didn't give Artus any magical powers in that regard. Still, he could think of one piece of advice Tyvian would probably have given him, if he were there.

Listen to the former Mage Defender, not the carpenter or the teenaged knight, you bloody dunce!

Artus couldn't help but laugh.

"I don't see what's funny," Barth said.

Artus controlled his expression. "No. We carry on as ordered. Myreon is right."

Barth's face darkened but he, too, got his expression under control. He bowed. "As my prince commands." He stomped out of the tent.

Valen watched the carpenter go. "You better hope she knows what she's doing. This army can't afford to lose a battle."

"Well, we'd better not let that happen, then."

CHAPTER 9

ON-THE-JOB TRAINING

The next few days saw the Ghouls take up a steady march overland, cutting across roads and farmland and woods without much care to the terrain. Captain Rodall set an ambitious pace for such uneven territory—anybody following them would have a hell of a time keeping up. As it was, they were only limited by the speed their supply wagons could make, and these were enhanced with wheels enchanted to make the progress relatively smooth. Tyvian wondered how many people would ever have guessed that the most expensive and useful tactical weapon available to the Ghouls was a bunch of wagon wheels.

Tyvian had a lot more time to think about things,

now that his role in the company had completely changed. He had gone from raw mercenary recruit to the indentured servant of Sahand's personal assassin overnight. He was not altogether certain it was a step up. For those first few days, Tyvian's duties were mostly sexual in nature. The rest of the time, however, Voth had him follow her around like some kind of lapdog, carrying her sword, her cape, her hat, or whatever else she didn't feel like burdening herself with. She trotted him around the camp like a trained pony. The looks he got from the men were a mixture of envy and pity—a grown man being bossed about by a slip of a woman? The Ghouls spat when they said his name . . . which was still Duchess.

Part of him—an old part, a deep part—wanted to challenge some of these hulking brutes to a duel or two, just to show them who was boss. Voth, though, had reminded him of just how thinly he was being tolerated by the captain. If he gave the Ghouls any excuse to run him through, he was good as dead. Rodall would have his head, and there wasn't a damned thing he could do about it.

So Tyvian held his tongue and endured the slights and kept his head down. And in the evenings, he had Voth all to himself. He told himself this was adequate compensation. And it almost was.

On the fourth day since the massacre at the village, the company came to a halt and set camp by the bend of a little stream that was flowing north. If

Tyvian's geography was as good as he'd hoped, they were close to the southern edge of Lake Country and the County of Hadda. Hadda was technically neutral in the conflict between the White Army and Sahand, but they wouldn't welcome Delloran boots on Hadda soil at all. At night, Tyvian could see the lights of a castle no more than two or three miles distant—the Ghouls' own campfires had to be visible to the castle, as well. Captain Rodall was announcing his presence, whereas before they had been moving so as to make it difficult for others to follow. This was a part of some larger game, but Tyvian couldn't guess at what. It was like trying to predict a *couronne* strategy by the location of a single piece.

That night, Tyvian tried to hold Voth in his arms, at least for a few moments. She twisted away, giving him a lopsided grin. "Now, now, Duchess—you don't want to give me the wrong idea, do you?"

"I assure you, I was merely offering to keep you warm a bit longer. A tiny little thing like yourself must freeze in these cool evenings."

Voth laughed and got dressed in a flowing silk robe of glossy black and embroidered with thread-of-gold. "My blood runs hotter than you think, Reldamar."

Tyvian lay back on the bed and thought of Myreon. He found himself thinking a lot about Myreon lately, particularly in this bed at times like this. Myreon would have stayed in his arms all night, holding him close. He would play with her strands of golden hair, feeling her breath push softly against his neck. He grimaced at the memory. He tried to think back, tried to pinpoint exactly where it had gone so wrong for the two of them. He couldn't think of one thing, but rather hundreds of little mistakes, of small little splinters that eventually killed whatever romance they had. Most of them were his fault, he was sure. *Gods, what a dunce I am.*

Voth snapped her fingers at him. "Hey, I don't like you like that."

"Like what?"

"Thinking. Your thinking tends to have fatal consequences."

"It isn't as though I'm given much else to do."

"Is that a complaint I detect? Surely not from the man whose life I saved from a grisly end?" Voth examined her dead white eye in a mirror, poking at it softly. She did this a lot. "Besides, I've got good news for you: your slate of duties is about to increase."

"And how's that?"

"You and I and Eddereon the Black and two others of the sergeant's recommendation are about to part company with the Ghouls and go on a little side-mission."

Tyvian sat up. "Who are the other two? What are we doing?"

"The men I think you know—two morons known as Hambone and Mort. The mission is, of course, still need-to-know."

"So what has this to do with me?"

Voth picked up a small vial of some kind of oil and poured a drop into her dead eye. "These men need to be brought up to speed with what we're going to be doing. I'm leaving the small unit tactics and such to Eddereon, but you I need to take over some of the more delicate aspects of their training."

Tyvian cocked his head. "Such as?"

"These men need to be able to pass for Eretherian knights."

Tyvian nodded. Those two words—*Eretherian knights*—were enough for him to put a number of pieces into place and establish context for a number of different things, not the least of which was why they were here, a scant few miles from Hadda's borders. He now knew what they were about to do—it should have been obvious, really, given Voth's talents. They were about to kidnap and murder someone, and Tyvian had a pretty short list of who that might possibly be.

All of them were friends.

The next day, those selected by Voth as members of her "team" were left with minimal supplies, two horses, and Voth's own tent. The rest of the Ghouls moved on, heading southwest. Witnessing it from the outside for the first time, he was surprised at how quickly the whole company was able to pick up and move. They were gone from sight before the sun had fully risen. Voth's little party was alone.

Mort, Hambone, and Tyvian were compelled to stand at attention while Eddereon went through any personal belongings the three of them had and presented them to Voth. Mort had a lock of hair from some mysterious brunette, some obviously shaved gambling dice, and an assortment of partially mummified chicken feet. Hambone had a smooth white rock, a compact Book of Hann with a flower pressed between the pages, and some brass knuckles. Tyvian had nothing whatsoever.

Voth eyed the pathetic little pile of mementos with a sardonic grin. She was standing on a large rock, her hands on her hips, as though she were about to give a stirring speech. She wasn't. "Easy duty's over, boys. It's time for some real work."

Mort shifted his lantern jaw back and forth. It made a cracking sound. "What we doing?"

Eddereon smacked him in the ribs with a swagger stick. "If she wants to hear you talk, she'll ask you a question!"

Mort remained at attention, but Tyvian could feel the huge man tense up beside him. "Easy, Mort," Tyvian whispered.

Voth kept talking. "Prince Banric has a mission for us. The details of that mission are none of your business. The purpose of that mission is none of your business. The only things that are your business are two facts: first, you do what I say, and second, if you don't do what I say, I'm allowed to kill you. We clear?"

Tyvian and his two companions nodded.

"Good." Voth hopped off the rock and headed toward her tent. "Each of you is going to come in here, one at a time, and we're going to get you out of those clothes." Tyvian half expected her to give him a wink at that last part, but she didn't. For the rest of the day, Voth was very businesslike.

Though Tyvian wasn't given the details, he had been involved in operations like this often enough that he could make a pretty good guess. The cover story would be this: Hambone and Mort would be masquerading as hedge knights who deserted the service of House Hadda in order to sign with the White Army. Tyvian and Eddereon would impersonate their squires, while Voth would be in the role of runaway farmgirl or similar—probably recently escaped from the ravages of Delloran soldiers. Desperate for experienced blades, the White Army would welcome them with open arms.

Then, once in the army, it was only a matter of finding a way to get close enough to whoever the target was to grab them, kill them, and vanish in the dead of night. Tyvian appreciated the tactical simplicity of the plan—armies on the march were confusing affairs, and everyone lived in tents. Slitting a throat in the night was very much within the bounds of plausibility.

All of it, though, relied upon Hambone and Mort making convincing hedge knights. Given that hedge knights tended to be filthy and poorly educated, Hambone and Mort had a head start in their preparations. The rest, though, was up to Tyvian.

During the day, Voth went out scouting and Eddereon ran the three of them through drills. These were mostly exercises in stealth and silent coordination. Tyvian had done things like this many times, and he found it fairly easy. Mort and Hambone were less able. They got an earful of Eddereon's gruff bark: "Hambone, why can't you have ankles like Duchess? Sounds like you're walking with a bone loose!"

Then, in the evenings, while Voth and Eddereon discussed tactics in her tent, Tyvian coached the two Dellorans in basic etiquette. On this particular evening, the challenge was eating with flatware.

Tyvian sat with a wooden tray across his knees on which were displayed a wedge of cheese and some strawberry preserves. The fork was an awkward wooden thing—gods knew where Voth had even found it—but Tyvian was able to spear a slice of cheese precisely, dip it in some of the preserves, and maneuver it into his mouth as smoothly as a pilot berthing a ship in his home port. "There, see? Easy."

Hambone was throttling his own fork like a broadsword. "Why can't we just use our hands? Don't rich folk use their hands?" He looked down at his own little platter of cheese and preserves, his forehead furrowed.

Mort had his fork held backward—as though intending to use it to murder someone in bed—and stabbed a piece of cheese with violent force. The tray shook and some of the preserves flew off and hit Hambone in the cheek. Tyvian winced. "Mort, it's cheese, not your mortal foe. More gently."

"I don't do things gently, Duchess," Mort growled. He bit the cheese off the end of his fork, teeth bare.

"If you don't do this gently, you'll likely wind up dead."

"Bah, what do you know?"

The expression on Hambone's face reminded him suddenly of Artus—particularly sullen Artus, when he was about fourteen and felt the world was devoted to his personal misery. He could see Artus scowling at him from across a campfire, rolling his eyes at his lesson. He remembered the boy's laughter; his bright, open face. The memory hurt somehow—so sharply that, for a moment, he looked at the ring. But no, that wasn't it. He only missed him. He only wished he could have spoken with him one more time.

"What's the matter with you, eh?" Mort was eating the cheese with his fingers now. The fork was nowhere to be seen.

"Mort, did you eat the fork, or are you just stupid?"

The big man rolled to his feet. "You want to say that again?"

Hambone stood up, too, and placed himself

between Tyvian and giant mercenary. "Hey, big man—take it easy. He's just following orders, right? It's what we're all doing, eh?"

"I don't like it when folks call me stupid," Mort said, more to Tyvian than to Hambone.

Tyvian remained seated. "Then perhaps you shouldn't do so many stupid things." He slowly tightened his grip on the fork. It might not be all that useful in hard cheese, but if Mort got too close, the big oaf was going to lose an eye.

Hambone patted Mort gently on his chest. "C'mon, Mort—the sergeant'll have your ears."

"Sergeant, my arse! His name's Ed, and he used to fart in our own tent."

Hambone laughed nervously. "You want to tussle with that old fighter? You heard the stories about him, right? Eddereon the Black . . ."

Mort, still glaring at Tyvian, backed off. "I'm going for a walk. Sleep with one eye open, Duchess—you hear?" He rolled his shoulders and backed away into the falling dusk.

Tyvian watched him go, shaking his head. "You know, Hambone—one of these days I'm afraid I'm going to have to stab that man."

Hambone turned around and forced a grin. Tyvian could tell the color had drained from his face a little—he was frightened. "Just like you done old Drawsher, eh?" He laughed, but it was too high-pitched to be genuine.

Gods, Tyvian thought, *he's afraid of me!*

Quiet fell between them. The crackle of the campfire complimented a soft chorus of crickets by the riverside. Somewhere, out there in the dark, they could hear Mort blundering around. At length, Tyvian cleared his throat. "Why'd you stand up for me?"

Hambone blinked and rubbed smoke from his eyes. "What?"

"The captain was going to kill you. Why step up for me? You could have held your tongue like everyone else. Why?"

Hambone got a stick and prodded at the fire. "Well, you and me are friends, ain't we?"

"I broke your knee with a shovel, Hambone."

Hambone shrugged. "I deserved it, right? Expect you'd done the same to ol' Mort, eh?"

Tyvian smiled. "You're learning, at least."

"See, what I don't get is this: How's a man who knows his way in a fight as well as you do—a man who can best a professional sell-sword like Drawsher—go all weak-kneed in battle? Hann's boots, Duchess—you was weeping like a girl. That part I ain't made up!"

Tyvian thought back to the village. It made him shudder. "You call that a battle, do you?"

"C'mon—you know what I mean."

Tyvian looked into the fire, trying to burn away the sounds of the screams, the smell of blood. "Here's what I don't understand, Ham. How's a fellow who stands up for his friends, who forgives them, who protects them from harm—how's he do what you did back in that village?"

"Do what?"

Tyvian scowled. "Don't make me say it. You know what you did."

"Oh." Hambone frowned. *That.* He paused, searching for the words, then shrugged. "Weren't everybody else doing it?"

"That's no kind of answer."

Hambone's expression darkened. The silence dragged out again. "I don't want to talk about this no more."

"Sure. Maybe you should just *think* about it, instead."

Voth came into the circle of firelight. She was dressed plainly—a woolen cloak, a peasant's dress, stained and dirty. A bloody bandage was bound across her dead eye. "Up." She pointed at Hambone. "Get into costume. Do you remember your heraldry?"

Hambone's jaw dropped open. He looked like he had been shot. "I . . . uhhhh . . ."

Voth rolled her good eye. "Kroth's teeth. Duchess, you stick close by this oaf and make sure he makes the right grunts at the right times or we'll all end up dead. Training time is over."

Tyvian stood up. "How close is the White Army?"

Voth's head snapped around, and she glared at him. After a moment, she laughed. "How much of the plan do you know already?" When Tyvian shrugged, she laughed again. "Just don't get any stupid ideas. I'll be watching you. Closely."

Tyvian made a courtly bow. This only made Voth laugh harder. "Gods, I *do* like you, Duchess. It will probably be the death of me, won't it?"

Tyvian smiled. "One can dream."

Eddereon had the horses saddled and Voth's tent packed up. Due to some Astral enchantments on it, it was unusually collapsible—small enough to be slung across the back of a saddle with little trouble. Mort and Hambone were each in mail, but of a higher quality than the stuff the Ghouls had issued. Where they had found a suit large enough to accommodate Mort's massive shoulders, Tyvian could only guess. None of his guesses seemed plausible.

The illusion of Mort and Hambone as Lake Country hedge knights on hard times was completed primarily by Eddereon and Tyvian, each of whom dressed in a tabard with the heraldic markings of their supposed masters. A good eye for heraldry would identify the two sell-swords as errant lances from somewhere in the Forest of Barrents, related very indirectly to the Earl of Barrentry on his mother's side, and from a largely disgraced corner of that line. Tyvian guessed the family names they were using as aliases hadn't been seen or heard of in the capital for at least two decades.

They set off south while it was still dark and rode until dawn. How they knew their way in the dark was a secret possessed by Eddereon alone, since he was in the lead. By the time the sun was up, Tyvian could see spirit engine tracks, cutting through the farmland like a black ribbon. That would put the Freegate Road to the west. How far indicated how far north they had come. If Tyvian had a slightly better eye for distances, he'd be able to pinpoint their exact location in Eretheria. As it was, he was reduced to the same kind of vague dead reckoning that had kept him alive before Hool had entered his life and travelling through the wilderness got a thousand times easier.

A wave of nostalgia threatened to overtake him yet again, and Tyvian stuffed it down before it could crest. What, was he supposed to live his life in regret now? Constantly moping for the old days? Tyvian felt that, more than anything else, was a sign of a man getting too old. *Hang the past. Focus on what's ahead. A new life. A new you.*

Thinking of Hool, though, did raise a concern. He walked ahead with Eddereon for a bit, scouting the land alongside the old Northron. "We may have a problem if we enter the camp. Hool—she could sniff me out."

Eddereon shook his head. "She's not with the White Army."

"How can you be so sure?"

"There is a trail of dead Dellorans stretching from here to beyond Ayventry that suggests your friend the gnoll has other plans. I overheard Captain Rodall discussing the reports on several occasions."

Despite himself, Tyvian smiled. "She's on a rampage. Avenging me."

Eddereon looked grave. "No. Not you." He turned and waved to Voth and the two "knights."

Tyvian's smile sank away. *Not me. Then who?*

Oh Gods—Brana . . .

For the rest of the morning, Tyvian's stomach felt tied in knots. Had he eaten anything, he might have thrown up.

They found the White Army shortly before midday. A troop of ragtag men in hunting greens came upon them from a copse of trees. When it became clear they weren't Dellorans and were travelling with a wounded peasant girl, they cheerfully informed them where the army could be found without any further questioning. "So much for security," Tyvian grumbled when they were out of earshot.

"Cheer up, Duchess," Voth said, "at least we didn't have to kill them."

Tyvian was holding Hambone's fraudulent banner aloft. He looked up at the "knight" to see he was pale and sweating. "I don't know about this," Hambone said.

"Shut the hell up," Mort growled. "You want to get us killed?"

"Both of you shut up!" Eddereon snapped. "Follow Duchess's lead."

The White Army was huge—twenty times or more larger than the Ghouls, judging from the number of tents. It was also twenty times more disorganized. Tyvian's brief stint in the Delloran army had shown him the militant precision Sahand expected of his bannermen and sell-swords—the army moved like a single organism or machine, oiled and seamless. The White Army seemed to be some kind of mass migration of angry men with spears. Tents were arrayed haphazardly, and other than a few masked men in white walking around who seemed to know what they were about, the rest of the army seemed uncertain whether they were meant to pack up camp, dig in, or practice marching.

"They need more sergeants," Eddereon said.

"The only thing they don't need more of is people," Tyvian countered, noting one group of men limping along without any shoes, their feet bloody and raw.

They had gone a good ways into the camp before they were stopped by a fellow in a dented breastplate and carrying a mace. He directed them to the quartermaster's tent, where they could "sign on."

The quartermaster was an older man, but built like a barn. He squatted on a stool and was hacking away in a ledger with a quill. Tyvian could tell from here that he was a man unaccustomed to writing.

When he saw them, he picked a pair of spectacles off his nose and folded them up. "More? Gods, it's turning into a busy day."

Tyvian bowed. "Sir, may I present Sir Hubert Macrole and his esteemed cousin, Sir Jorris Dalvert, both of the Forest of Barrents."

The quartermaster wiped ink off his fingers by rubbing them on his sleeve and extended a hand to shake. "Gammond Barth. I'm a carpenter, but you'd best get used to shaking my hand anyway." He grinned.

Tyvian shook—the old man had a grip like a vise. Tyvian looked up at the two Dellorans and gave them a hard stare. Mort was the first to react. "We've come to kill Dellorans."

"Then you're in good company. We'll be happy to give you the chance, just as soon as we find some." Barth laughed. No one else did.

It was now Hambone's line. "Oh! Uhhh . . . we . . . we've got some smarts!"

"*Intelligence* . . ." Tyvian coughed.

Hambone's cheeks reddened. "Right—intelligence. About Tor Erdun!"

Barth stopped laughing and looked serious. "Truly, son? You're not telling tall tales, are you? We had our fill of those, understand? We'll throw you out if you're lying, horses and armor or no."

Voth made a good show of looking shy as she

came forward and curtsied. Just watching her performance made Tyvian's ring clamp down. "Please, sir—I'm the one what told them. I'm from Tor Erdun. The Dellorans killed my father. He . . . he was a miller . . ." Tears welled in her good eye. Her body shook. The effect was perfectly realized. Though he knew it was a lie, even Tyvian felt moved.

Barth put his arm around her. "Oh, you poor thing. Come on, come on—let's get you something to eat and you can tell me all about it."

"You want us to stay?" Mort asked, though it was somewhat unclear who he was asking—Barth or Voth.

Barth shook his head. "She's in good hands, lads—you've done well. Get yourself settled and come back in a bit. I want to hear her story first and then yours later. All right?"

Mort and Hambone exchanged glances. "Yeah . . . uhhh . . . okay." Hambone shrugged. He scooted in his saddle, as though willing the horse to back up but not being really sure how to do that.

Tyvian grabbed the bridle before anything untoward could occur. "We'll leave her in your capable care. Our thanks."

Voth and Barth disappeared inside the tent. If Voth's target was the White Army's quartermaster, that man was as good as dead. He had a sense it wasn't, though. Looking around at the chaos of the White Army's camp, it was pretty clear that the quartermaster was *not* Myreon's primary military asset. It only remained to be seen who was.

"That went well!" Hambone observed, smiling.

Mort was more pensive. "Ain't over yet, Ham."

Tyvian grimaced at the failure to use Hambone's alias. "Come on—let's find somewhere to pitch this tent."

CHAPTER 10

THE JAWS OF VENGEANCE

The Delloran patrol had not died quickly. Though Hool had come upon them unawares, they were good fighters and tough, for humans. But there were only eight of them, and two of them had been sleeping.

And none of them could see in the dark.

At dawn, Sir Damon Pirenne—now just "Damon"—joined her in the ruins of the little camp where it stood beneath a dead tree on the slopes of a windswept hill somewhere around the place where Eretheria ended and Galaspin began. As usual, he was nervous around the bodies. Especially the ones Hool had impaled on tree branches. He rubbed his